KASE INGLLLS

THE STEPPING CREEK

Copyright © 2024 by Kase Ingalls
All rights reserved.

No part of this publication may be reproduced, distributed, or transmitted in any form or by any means, including photocopying, recording, or other electronic or mechanical methods, without the prior written permission of the publisher, except as permitted by U.S. copyright law.

Without in any way limiting the author's exclusive rights under copyright, any use of this publication to "train" generative artificial intelligence (AI) technologies to generate text is expressly prohibited. The author reserves all rights to license uses of this work for generative AI training and development of machine learning language models.

For permission requests, contact: ingallskase@gmail.com.

The story, all names, characters, and incidents portrayed in this production are fictitious. No identification with actual persons (living or deceased), places, buildings, and products is intended or should be inferred.

Book Cover by My Lan Khuc (LaolanArt)

Edition Number: 1 Publication Date: 2024

"If I search among my memories for those whose taste is lasting, if I write the balance sheet of the moments that truly counted, I surely find those that no fortune could have bought me. You cannot buy the friendship of a companion bound to you forever by ordeals endured together."

— Antoine de Saint-Exupéry, Wind, Sand and Stars

Chapter 1

The morning sun had barely edged above the mountains to the east of the deep valley several thousand feet below him. But the light was brilliant, almost blinding as it reflected in the turbulent water of the narrow mountain stream. The light seemed to scatter in the nearby inky shadows of the forest as it bounced off the tumbling water which surged and fell back over the polished rocks, carrying the energy of the upper mountain snowpack far above. The stream water was cold but the warmth of the sun was finding its way into its shallows. The sun's path moved up the nearby mountains, slowly, but with increasing brilliance and warmth, opening the gates to a day that was unfolding with promise and trust—the trust that comes with the bold potential of belief in spite of anything tangible to support it.

Craig Kelly knelt and cupped his hands in the creek, and took one final drink of the cold water. He swung his small grey rucksack onto his back and jumped the three feet to the other bank and walked into the dense forest. The branches hundreds of feet above him were filtering the sunlight and columns of light and darkness fell on the forest floor. The columns of light appeared to travel with Kelly as he moved easily between the trees and brush, with unhurried purpose.

The actual physical location that was his world at this moment, for as long as this moment might last – and that was decidedly uncertain—was stunning in beauty and also in its scale. The mountains seemed to not have a final place where any reasonable person would call an end. They just kept going the same way a desert highway does when you lay down flat in the middle of it and set your gaze on its straight and endless path. The mountains were jagged at their highest points and snow filled in the chutes and couloirs, stacked high on airy rock ledges in spite of the sun and gravity. The snow stretched downward for several thousand feet below the highest peaks. It was still fairly early in spring, with days that were stretching out and getting warmer. But the nights were still cold here above 6000 feet.

No single event had landed Kelly here. It was a series of acts, many cards drawn from an inscrutable deck, an alchemy that could have never been mapped out. All of the acts intersecting at distant points, far from their origins. It all lay outside even the wildest imagination. Like so many junctures that chart a course where the unknown pieces far outnumber those that are visible, the events that delivered him alone and deep into these high peaks were especially random in both variety and irony—with pieces of both good and bad luck. He was for now, by the hand of fate, a gypsy.

It had started with a letter from his friend, Tommy Dickson, hand-delivered to Kelly at his small cabin near Ao Thong Yee Beach in southern Thailand, a still mostly undiscovered part of the country where he had decided to live until he felt compelled to leave. The person who handed it to him was a girl from Sweden. The first time he had seen her, she was tending a bar at a cafe about half-a-mile down from his cabin. He'd gone to the bar just after sunset to ask if anyone had found a book that he had left behind two days earlier. The waitress told him to check with Ana, and nodded toward the bar.

Kelly glanced at the girl behind the bar. She was naturally beautiful, with striking features and long hair falling over her shoulders. She moved easily while doing the work of mixing drinks and looking after the customers—mostly men—who were gathered at the bar seeking her attention.

With little deliberation, Kelly decided not to compete with them. He could replace the book, he decided. He walked toward the door, moving aside for a young couple entering the bar. He glanced once more in the girl's direction. She was bending down and filling a glass with ice. At that moment she looked up and her eyes caught Kelly's. Her stare was unflinching and her eyes were so beautiful that Kelly forgot briefly why he had come into the bar. Then she stood up and turned away.

Kelly turned and walked out of the bar. He stepped into the fading light of the evening and onto the warm sand of the beach, the loud chatter of the bar fading behind him to a soft hum. The air was warm and still, and the sound of small waves falling onto the sand drifted gently up the beach. Kelly noticed the moon was almost full and its light was already reflecting off the ocean, giving the evening a feeling of shrouded daylight but the embrace of approaching night. The image of the girl's soft but penetrating eyes and her graceful movements were fixed in his mind, whether he wanted them there or not.

Kelly walked down closer to the water, removed his shirt and kicked off his rubber sandals. He left them in a neat pile in the sand and made his way to the water. He eased his way into it, pushing gently against the surge of the small waves until the water came to his chest and then he began swimming in easy, steady strokes. The ocean was calm beyond the small waves falling on the beach and it was lit by the moon.

Kelly swam straight out for several hundred feet and then turned back, swimming toward two palm trees whose trunks crossed near their tops. The trees were just up the beach from where he had left his shirt and sandals.

As he swam, he lifted his head toward the palms and a reflection from the beach caught his eye. A small piece of tin or glass was reflecting the moonlight, he thought. Maybe a bottle. But the reflection was steady as Kelly swam. And it was directly down from the palms.

He saw that the light was coming from a flashlight of some kind when he reached the shallow part of the water and began walking toward the dry sand. He stepped out of the ocean and began walking toward the light—it was a headlamp and from the light Kelly saw the silhouette of a girl with long hair. The light was reflecting off pages of a book that she held in her hands and then closed as he approached.

"That was you that left behind the book?" she said. It was more of a comment than a question. But Kelly felt the question echo into his future and he knew he would answer it.

"Yes."

"Do you always read that type of book?"

She was sitting in the sand next to his sandals, her arms crossed over her bended knees. In the moonlight Kelly could see the gentle brilliance of her eyes.

She handed the book to him, *The Old Man and The Sea,* by Ernest Hemingway.

"I'm Ana," she said, extending her hand.

"I'm Craig," Kelly said, as he shook her hand. "Thank you for delivering my book."

"You like Hemingway?" she asked.

"I like the honesty of his stories but I don't always like the stories themselves...but I like this one," Kelly said, nodding to the book lying next to Ana in the sand.

Ana noticed his dark hair, still wet from his swim. It glistened slightly in the moonlight when he turned his head toward her. She guessed he was about 32 years old. She had watched him walk up the beach and had thought from his powerful build and the way he had moved easily and confidently in the soft sand that he was an athlete; a professional skier or soccer player came to her mind.

"I always thought Hemingway was a little full of himself," Ana said. "That's what I heard from American women, but I read part of your book and I liked it. So, I think I can give Hemingway a chance."

Kelly laughed. "Where are you from," he asked.

"I'm Swedish," Ana said.

"Do you ski?" Kelly asked.

"I ski when I'm in the mountains, but lately I've been doing a lot of running on the beach. I left Sweden two years ago and travelled across Europe and Asia and parts of the American west. And then I found my way here six months ago. I felt comfortable here so I decided to stay for a while."

"I think we should go running sometime," Kelly said.

"We can go running but you'll have to keep up with me," she said, laughing softly.

"I'll keep up," Kelly said, smiling warmly.

The sun was filling in the sky to the east by the time they finished sitting on the beach together, sometimes talking and listening to each other, sometimes just sitting with each other. Then they made their way to the café for coffee.

Kelly saw Ana everyday over the next two months, except for the few days she went to visit friends in the bigger city to the west.

He was sitting on his small deck when she walked up the bamboo plank steps of his cabin and handed him the letter. Her legs were tanned and athletic. Her blond hair was brilliant in the morning light and the plan Kelly had for taking a small boat out this morning to explore a small island vanished from his mind. Kelly didn't trust perfection, he didn't like how it somehow refuted what might reveal itself from another try, from the courage of continual perseverance. But he knew when he saw Ana walk up the steps to his cabin that he was alive in a place that needed nothing else.

"You have received something from the US. Maybe from a friend?" she said as she handed him the worn letter.

"How did someone find me here?" Kelly said.

"The same way I found you. You just have to know where to look."

Ana Jonen was 28 years old. It was restlessness that had sent her away from Sweden and when she decided to stay in Thailand that restlessness was somehow gone. She was content with the routine provided by a steady address and she liked the pace of the small beach community. But she sensed that her contentment had been shaken when she met Kelly, and the familiar restlessness had stirred in her again—though it felt different to her this time.

She took a seat in the high-backed wicker chair next to Kelly, the one he had written her name on in a deep red-orange paint given to him by a local fisherman.

"Do I own this chair now?" she asked with a laugh as she sank back on the worn slats. She wore loose-fitting, faded red nylon shorts and a white, long-sleeved button-down shirt with a black bikini top underneath. Her long, straight hair fell over her chest.

"You look good in that chair," Kelly said. "It's absolutely your chair."

Kelly got up and went inside his small hut to make coffee. He set the letter on a short table next to Ana.

Ana kicked off her leather sandals and stretched her legs out on the deck. She felt the sun fall onto them. A light breeze came up the beach from the ocean as she watched several small sea birds fly low over the water and then swoop skyward for several hundred feet before diving sharply for the waves. She closed her eyes and listened as another breeze came off the ocean and rushed softly into the wing-like branches of the palm tree beside the hut.

She heard Kelly step back onto the deck. He set a fresh mug of coffee on the table next to her and eased into the chair beside her.

They stayed on the deck for two hours, drinking coffee and talking about mountain ranges, favorite books, climbing in the American west, and skiing in Sweden and Norway. Then they listed the best swimming beaches along the river that ran into the large bay a mile down the beach.

When they had finished talking, they went for a run down that beach and, after about a mile, ran into the jungle to swim in one of those spots they had talked about. Then Ana had to leave to start work at the restaurant.

"If that letter takes you away, just give me one good clue, a spot on the map, before you leave," she said as she broke into an easy jog up the beach, waving her hand above her head. She turned to give Kelly a quick look over her shoulder, her long blond hair falling down her back.

The letter would take him away and Ana somehow knew that. She had glanced at the postage stamps on the letter, an image of the Purple Heart Medal. Ana sensed a greater meaning in that choice of stamp by the person who had written the letter, even though Kelly had not mentioned military service during the weeks they had spent together.

Kelly glanced at the return address of the letter and saw that it was from his friend Tommy Dickson. They had known each other since their first day of army training. They became friends during several months of life entirely scripted by a training curriculum. By luck, they were later assigned to the same infantry unit and had served as Rifle Platoon Leaders together shortly after their country entered into a decades-long conflict in Afghanistan. They had become friends quickly during their training schools, bound by their shared interest in rock climbing and surfing. They also shared an independent view of the world. And that sometimes meant they carried with them a subtle irreverence for the tedium and formality of army training. To some of their peers, notably those who considered military training as sacred as religion, they were an enigma. To their instructors they were simply the two trainees who most often exceeded the standard for leadership qualities, physical fitness and academia.

So, the two young men proceeded with little difficulty through the gauntlet of their various training programs until they could graduate and enter the much less formal and decidedly more results-oriented world of a line infantry unit. Their friendship became a transcendent bond under the crucible of combat and coming to the edge of their own mortality. The US military had redefined for them what normal and reasonable living is and how long a person with average luck might be able to sustain it.

When they were both promoted to Captain—a ceremony completed in ten minutes in the still morning heat of a remote desert in Africa, they had clinked their coffee cups together to celebrate. Five minutes later they began inspecting their weapons and loading their magazines for another mission.

Kelly read the letter later that night when Ana was working.

Hi Craig. Are you enjoying your freedom, some leisure living? I think you'd be better off in the desert. Can you start mid-March? Two-month commitment. You can see the mountains from the compound and run on endless, empty trails. The food is above average. Everybody here is capable. Let me know soon. Regards. TD.

Chapter 2

He and Dickson had lived day-to-day during their combat tours and relied on each other to stay alive and keep their soldiers alive while escaping and re-entering dangerous places. They had witnessed heroism and tragedy almost daily. When they had started making their way in the civilian world, the most remarkable and surprising challenge for them had been confronting routine social interaction. They had both struggled with it, especially when they found themselves at things like backyard barbecues, or weddings. The small talk that others engaged in so easily usually left Kelly and Dickson in silence, unable to bring themselves to participate. Most of the time they simply walked away as the people around them followed them with puzzled eyes.

Dickson chose to create distance between himself and potential social engagements by simply disappearing. He took a two-year tour of remote beaches and isolated surf breaks in Asia, then went sailing on the west coast of the United States before finding his way back to the military as a private contractor. When he wrote to Kelly, he was providing a technical review of training exercises in urban areas; those mock scenarios that the military designed—and made as realistic as possible—to test the readiness of its soldiers and equipment. In this case the review was being carried out in the Utah desert within a web-like cluster of buildings, houses and roads that the military had constructed to resemble the kind of village you might find in Africa or Afghanistan.

The military was not only evaluating small teams of soldiers, but also new ways of fighting in urban combat scenarios, such as house-to-house fighting. Dickson's employer was a manufacturer of systems that integrated drones with computer software used by soldiers.

Kelly had given himself the freedom to not think about military tactics and his many combat missions when he left the military, but even with that the solace he had hoped for as a civilian seemed more elusive to him than it had been for Dickson. Before he landed in Thailand, Kelly had spent a few months in western US and Canada, most of the time in and around the mountains and rivers of the Pacific Northwest, where he had grown up.

He had paid cash for a low-mileage campervan whose owners had abandoned Van Life for an apartment in Ballard, Washington. He determined the van was built-out with excess accessories and comfort, and therefore had been missing its true purpose for existing. So he removed the cabinets and table, swivel chairs and the TV and loaded the van with food and water, climbing gear, a sleeping bag, three rucksacks, clothing, stove and tent, skis and two surfboards. He left Ballard and embarked on several long road trips throughout the western US and Canada, stopping to ski, climb or surf. The freedom and independence of the life suited him. He surfed in undiscovered places and climbed alone among the remote Cascade Mountain peaks. He swam in rivers and lakes and watched the sun rise from places few people had ever been. Being alone nourished his need for independence, but after several months he began feeling isolated and too aware of not being able to share the majesty and beauty of the places he had ventured into. So, he soon found himself back in his old home town Redmond, Washington, trying to figure out what he was good at, and if he even fitted in with the world that had raised him.

In those first months back home, Kelly was asked by a friend of a friend to speak about his military experience to a group of mid-level managers at a sporting goods convention. It was being held in Redmond, making it harder for Kelly to say no. But initially he *did* say no. It struck him that this group would be unable to relate to his experience and translate it into their work, as the mutual friend believed it would for no tangible reason that Kelly could understand. But the friend kept nagging him. After a month of refusals, Kelly finally relented and said yes, mostly to help his friend out.

The memory of those 40 minutes was still clear in Kelly's mind months later. A spacious conference room where he stood off to the side next to a high wall. A hundred conference goers were seated in neat rows, most of them wearing shorts and colorful polo shirts. Kelly liked the spaciousness of the room and the potential of learning something from the audience. But he couldn't help being reminded of tourists dressed for golf or dinner while vacationing in Hawaii or Mexico. They chatted excitedly among themselves as a formally dressed man, standing on the stage at the front, waited patiently for the talking to settle, apparently hoping his presence would signal a shift in decorum and the start of the event. Two men seated in the last row were throwing a miniature orange football back and forth to their friends. Kelly couldn't help but notice it and he realized things might not go well for him. But he had accepted the invitation and prepared for the presentation, so he told himself he had to give it a chance.

The man on the stage, thin and wiry and bald except for thick drapes of dark hair on each side of his head, was wearing blue slacks that seemed out of place with the sandals on his feet. He leaned into the microphone on the lectern and said something about how much he enjoyed these events, apparently to signal to the audience that things were now underway. The chatter only grew louder. The speaker—who clearly was not enjoying himself – glanced anxiously at Kelly. After another failed attempt to quiet the crowd, the man demanded the attention of the audience in a high-pitched, half-scream. The drone of chatter abruptly fell to awkward silence. Kelly hoped the audience might be able to redeem itself. He was going to give it that chance.

He came to the stage and began speaking and, after briefly describing his background and his job in the US Army, he recounted his experiences leading small units, trying to frame leadership in useful ways for the audience. The audience seemed to be listening closely, between sips of coffee and bites of donuts, and Kelly hoped the next 20 minutes might turn out OK. After a few more minutes, he began taking questions.

"How did you spend the weekends?" A pudgy man in his thirties asked this first question. Kelly paused, expecting some laughter. But it never came. So he answered simply that the day of the week in a combat zone was unimportant, as everything was driven by missions completed and those that were coming next. The audience seemed disappointed. The next person asked how many calories soldiers need on a typical day in a combat zone. "At least that's an improvement," Kelly thought to himself.

But then the next question came—from an anxious, stocky man standing in shorts and a tee shirt: "How many times did someone try to kill you?"

Kelly was silent for several seconds, as though calculating a number in his mind. "Several thousand times," he finally answered, with no hint of sarcasm.

"Really?" the questioner responded. "Is that true?"

"I have no idea if that's true," Kelly said.

A silence fell onto the room as the stocky man remained standing. Then a few people in the front row laughed nervously.

"But you just said it was true," the stocky man said, looking at others around him and attempting to solicit support for his inquiry.

"I never said it was true," Kelly said. "But it is entertaining."

The stocky man looked confused, but his demeanor quickly turned to agitation. His short, gelled hair took on a shiny gleam under the room's overhead lights, which now appeared more intense.

"It seems like it's something you would have kept track of, something that's important," the man said, now in a challenging tone.

The audience hushed. The questioner, still standing, resolute in the rightness of his question, was demanding an answer to confirm he had raised something vital. And maybe he was also trying to avoid being embarrassed, as he sensed that was now a possibility. The nervous event coordinator seated in the front row felt the tension sweep over the silent audience. Someone in the back of the room half-coughed involuntarily.

But Kelly was not nervous as he looked out from the stage and only saw the large room. A thin woman in the front row thought he looked unnaturally relaxed and it caused a pang of anxiety to strike her. She wondered what would happen next.

Kelly looked detached as his gaze went to the back corner of the room, where he saw a side door propped open, the August afternoon sunshine spilling in. It suddenly struck him that it was a beautiful day. The audience waited for him to respond but his thoughts were no longer with them or the question that had been directed at him. He remained silent. Two waiters in the back of the room who were bringing in coffee and snacks, saw him and stopped what they were doing. The nervous event coordinator stood up and started to walk to the stage. But then he thought better of it, turned around and sat back down.

The stocky man, now emboldened, turned again to the audience in a short jerky movement.

"My question needs an answer!" he shouted, with a dramatic wave of his arms.

But the speed of his turn outmatched his agility as one of his sandals caught the front leg of his chair. The thin rubber sole twisted under his foot, and instead of an answer from Kelly he got a loud gasp from the audience as his overburdened center of gravity sent him crashing over his chair and into the row behind him. His fall took out two chubby women in loose, printed dresses who likewise sent their morning lattes backwards into the next row, eliciting more gasps and a few scattered screams.

※ ※ ※

As Craig Kelly walked off the stage, past the audience and out the open door into the warm afternoon sunshine, he looked as though he was strolling along a beach.

The conference center happened to be across from a city park with neatly kept green soccer fields that ran along the shoreline of a large lake with a sandy beach. Kelly remembered this beach from his childhood—the long expanse of sand and the gradual slope of the shoreline. It was where he would swim with his friends whenever they could persuade a parent or older sibling to drive them there.

Without pausing, Kelly walked across the soccer fields to the beach, where he removed his shoes, socks and shirt. The warm sand on his bare feet had never felt better as he rolled up his pant legs, dove into the lake, and began swimming. The cold water felt shocking at first but it urged him forward into powerful strokes. Soon his body generated its own warmth, his heart pumping blood to his limbs, each stroke and kick bringing him closer to a synchronization of warmth and solace that he always received from physical exertion.

He reached the far shore after ten minutes of steady swimming, then started back. The lake was calm and unusually empty of boats or other swimmers. His powerful body generated a steady and even wake that was the only disturbance across the surface of the water. A group of ducks slowly paddled away from him as he swam in their direction. He could still feel the warmth of the sun on his face as it moved in and out of the water.

Kelly's hands felt the sandy bottom before he realized he was at the shore. He brought his legs under him and stood up. Then he began walking to the shore, pushing against the water at his waist. He looked to the beach and saw a little girl running toward him, kicking a soccer ball. As he stepped out of the water and onto the sand, she kicked the ball to him.

She was about seven years old, barefoot, and wearing soccer shorts and a baseball cap that came down over her ears. Two pigtails of sun-bleached light-brown hair fell onto her shoulders.

"I saw you out there swimming. I'm going to swim in the lake today for the first time!" she said proudly.

"I bet you're a great swimmer!" Kelly replied. He kicked the ball back to her and she picked it up and began tossing it in the air and catching it.

"Where are your parents?" Kelly said. "You can't go in there by yourself."

"My mom is over there," the girl said, pointing to a woman in her thirties sitting farther up on the beach. Kelly looked in the direction of the woman, who waved at them. Kelly and the girl waved back.

"You get a high five for swimming so far," the girl said to Kelly, as she raised her hand. Kelly put his hand out and the girl gave it a solid clap. They both laughed

"Why were you out there swimming by yourself?" the girl said.

"My friends are all somewhere else today," Kelly answered.

"If they were here I bet they would be swimming with you," the girl said.

"I bet you're right."

With that, she turned and ran up the beach towards her mother, kicking the soccer ball along the way. "See you later!" she yelled, turning to wave at Kelly, who waved back.

As he collected his shoes and shirt from the sand, Kelly's mind was flooded with images of playing and swimming with his friends at this beach. As he walked across one of the soccer fields to his car a warm gust of wind descended from a cluster of maple trees that lined the field. He felt the soft grass on his bare feet as the breeze swept over him and rose back up toward the trees, rustling in the leaves that were dappled with the sun's brilliance. When Kelly got to his car, he was thinking about where he could buy a pair of swimming goggles. A week later he flew to Thailand.

Chapter 3

It took Kelly a few days to decide to go to the Utah desert to work with his friend, though deep down he knew he would go when he first read the letter. He and Dickson knew that the most important part of Dickson's message was, *Everyone here is competent.* Their combat experience had stripped away any attention they could give to things that did not have a coherent and important goal, or to people who were not capable of achieving one. Kelly was determined to stay away from those people as much as he could.

Kelly said yes to the job because he still felt an obligation to his country and he believed that the work his friend was doing was important. The money wasn't critical, but it would certainly help fund his next trip, the exact location was as yet unknown, but he knew it would be expensive to get to and he planned to stay there for a year.

So it was that Craig Kelly found himself perched on the edge of an old leather office chair next to the open door of a sturdy, wooden-framed hut in the Utah desert southwest of Salt Lake City. The predictable cool evening breeze had started to push across the broad valley, carrying the cool mountain air down from the snow-covered Wasatch peaks. Kelly sat semi-rigid, focused intently on a small notebook that sat on a grey metal government desk as he replayed the events of the day in his mind. His left elbow was resting on the corner of the desk, his hand poised above it seemingly held by an invisible wire, the hand and fingers clenched around a pen working at his command and also holding something that was not as his command, the tension of the memories of combat and being close to death. The pen moved quickly to the notebook, making edits and adding details to the pages, then back to its place of suspension.

At last Kelly finished the editing and sighed heavily. He placed the pen on the desk, becoming aware of the tightness of the muscles and tendons in his hand. He looked down and saw his fingers were clenched and two of them were twitching. He took several long, slow deep breaths. It helped a little. It usually did.

The leather chair looked out of place in the hut. He'd first seen it in a dusty parking lot at a roadside thrift shop in a nearby desert town whose total population was smaller than the roster of a major college football team. The chair was comfortable and he'd bought it thinking it could find a new purpose in his hut in this vast military training area in the middle of the desert. The desert sand had already found a permanent home in the chair's cracked leather creases. Everything else in the hut—duffle bags, cots, foot lockers, even the cloth, netted window screens – was olive drab green or gray and conveyed the simplicity of military order and resiliency. The chair was a relic, but it had endured by virtue of its utility. It was perfect, he thought.

The day had started cool but by noon it had the penetrating warmth of early spring sun. Kelly had spent the morning observing and documenting how well the teams had been able to use images from drones to operate in teams of seven within a small cluster of buildings as they searched for "enemy" soldiers. They were discovering what worked and what problems developed with the drones and transmitting images and how teams naturally adapted as they moved among buildings, where everything was a potential trap; hallways, hidden stairs, the rooftop. Not everything worked as it should this day, as was usually the case. Kelly was keeping detailed notes relevant to the critical lessons, the chain of events and decisions when things went wrong, and the subsequent actions of individuals and units.

He finished his work, got a beer from the small cooler inside the hut, and stepped outside into the cool breeze. Everything was peaceful here, he thought. It had the quiet calm of an empty, remote beach. The distractions from the bigger civilized world, which he still visited often, were absent. He brought a small folding chair from inside his hut and sat down to gaze at the distant snow-covered mountain range. He opened the cold beer, took a sip and set it on the ground. Then he stretched his legs out in front of him, kicking off his sandals and sliding his bare feet across the warm sand.

"It looks like the desert suits you," said Dickson, who had walked up behind him. He had come from a small cluster of buildings a quarter mile away near the main dirt road leading to the compound. Dickson was tall with dark hair and slightly awkward when he was forced to move slowly. But when he quickened to his natural swift pace, he had the easy agility of an athlete. His jet-black hair fell just over his ears and he had the windblown, tanned appearance of an itinerant surfer, or a happy nomad.

Kelly looked up and smiled at his friend.

"I'm getting used to the view. Mountains make sense, like they belong there," said Kelly.

"Unlike other things, you mean, like cities?"

"That's exactly what I mean."

"I wonder what that would be like – America without cities and cars and highways," said Dickson.

"It would be like this," replied Kelly. "Grab a chair and we can think about other ways America could look different. But not too much. Thinking too much is usually a bad strategy."

Dickson pulled up a chair and took a beer from the cooler.

"You have some mail," he said, as he handed Kelly a faded and creased hand-drawn card with the image of a long, tropical beach on the front.

"Who found me out here in the middle of the desert?" Kelly said.

"I'd say a girl who is smarter than you," Dickson answered, laughing.

"She's smarter and also faster," Kelly said glancing at the card. He turned it over and saw a finely sketched map with a road leading from the town of San Vito di Cadore to a small building with the letter A next to it. The building was in a valley below a mountain peak, Forcella Grande. In the margin of the map was written, *Starting Sept 1. Come find me xo AJ.*

"She just drew you a topo map... I'd say it's somewhere in the Italian Dolomites," Dickson said.

"It's a clue," Kelly said.

"Hidden treasure?"

"It's where she's living."

"That's even better. You probably need to find your way to that spot on the map when you're done here."

"I do need to find my way to that spot. I think I'm going to do that," Kelly said.

The two friends sat in silence, gazing toward the distant mountains, neither of them feeling the need to interrupt the stillness. Behind them the cloth window screen gently flapped in the breeze.

Dickson finally broke the silence. "There's good views in Canada, too."

Kelly looked over at his friend. "I'm sure there are but I just sat down a few minutes ago and I'm pretty comfortable."

"The training team in the Northern Rockies needs some help."

Kelly lowered his beer and sighed.

"One of the analysts had an allergic reaction to a bee sting," Dickson went on. "And he's probably done for the next two weeks at least. Wanna go live in real mountains for a month?"

Kelly looked at his friend skeptically. "I was just adjusting to the desert air," he said.

"The training site is not far from the Bugaboo Mountains. I told them you'd probably go if you could sneak away for a few days of hiking and running after a week-long stint. They said they'd get you to any trailhead of your choice. They have real beer up there, too."

Kelly smiled. "You've already done the negotiating for me? That's slightly troubling. I'm not sure I like being so predictable."

"Predictable only to your good friends. To the world you remain an enigma."

"Thank God. When do I need to be up there?"

"We can get you on a fixed wing that's already headed that way tomorrow morning. You fly into Banff and then it's a two-hour drive to the training site."

"Just like that, I'm off to Canada. One pissed off Canadian bee and I'm headed into the mountains."

"Canadian bees only sting Americans, according to the locals."

Kelly laughed and picked up his beer. "I'll have to wear one of those maple leaf flags on my jacket," he said.

Chapter 4

When the next morning arrived, the air was unusually still. There was no hint of a breeze and the usual sounds of the birds that typically came to visit and announce their presence among the compound's scattered tents were absent.

The sun's first rays had begun spilling over the Wasatch Mountains to the northeast, spreading across the desert and onto the cool asphalt of the remote military airstrip. Kelly appeared to be the lone living creature in a vast expanse of sand and juniper as he walked casually in lightweight nylon pants and a t shirt across the airstrip apron to a twin-engine turbo prop plane parked just off the single runway. He entered the aircraft, dropped a duffle bag and rucksack on the floor near the middle of the plane, and took a seat in the back.

A few minutes later Kelly heard the pilot climb up the steps of the plane. He saw him step into the cockpit briefly. He then walked into the cabin where Kelly was seated. Kelly recognized the calm demeanor, the steadiness of an experienced military pilot that he had seen so many times while riding in the back of helicopters and fixed wing planes in combat zones. The pilot was wearing jeans and a lightweight green jacket. His hair was wavy and dark brown and combed straight back. It fell below his ears. He looked to be about forty, had a goa-tee and mustache and a couple weeks of beard growth. Kelly wondered if they had ever been in the same aircraft together in another part of the world.

"Make yourself at home, you're the only passenger," the pilot said. With that he turned and walked back to the cockpit.

Ten minutes later, the pilot was taxiing the plane to the end of the runway. He smoothly turned into a rolling takeoff, sending the aircraft quickly down the pavement and into the air, leaving the ground so easily that to Kelly it seemed like an illusion. The plane immediately began climbing toward the high mountain ranges to the north.

Getting dressed that morning, with his packed duffel bag and the small rucksack lying next to him on the plywood floor, Kelly had marveled at his now empty hut. He pondered his nomadic existence, staying for brief periods in a series of residences, where everything that he needed could be packed for travel in 30 minutes. Living this way allowed him a lot of freedom. Displacement had become his normalcy. It wasn't for everyone, he knew, but it suited him.

He had gathered the last two items—a water bottle and a headlamp—on the small table in the hut, and slipped his feet into his sandals for the flight to Canada. His comfort in dressing so casually was something he treated with almost religious ceremony. He had not rushed dressing; in the same way other people don't rush their prayers. He had served so long under the requirements of prescriptive dress, which usually came with gear and equipment to be worn or carried, that putting on casual civilian clothes was for him a kind of emancipation. So he resented it slightly when an uninvited thought suddenly interrupted his meditation: *routine things go wrong sometimes, and for no apparent reason.* He knew it was impossible to decipher these cautionary voices he sometimes heard, or to distinguish them from simple fear—but he had learned to obey them if they didn't impose a significant burden. He removed the sandals, put on socks and slid his feet into his worn leather and canvas jungle boots.

As the plane continued its climb, Kelly settled into his seat in the airplane, stretched his legs out in front, and reclined the seat back as far as it would go. He reached into the rucksack that sat on the seat next to him, pulled a book from it, and began reading the account of a solo around-the world sailing journey, completed in 1898 without the benefit of an engine. The complete self-reliance of the sailor had drawn Kelly to the book, which he had found in a used bookstore in a small town in eastern Montana – over 700 miles from the ocean.

Kelly was absorbed in the book, occasionally looking up from the pages to glance out the window. In just 30 minutes, the landscape below had changed from arid desert to thick forest to steep, mountain peaks and snowfields. The flight was calm and routine; the pilot steady and focused in his task of flying, while Kelly sat alone and at peace in the cabin. The aircraft itself moved through the sky with ease and remarkable smoothness. The tranquility, Kelly thought briefly, seemed unusual. Things were rarely this effortless. But he pushed the thought away, attributing it to a life so often spent working in a chaotic environment. He went back to his book. But a few minutes later, he felt a slight vibration ripple through the floor, a barely detectable tremor in the sole of his boots. He instinctively closed the book and put it on the seat beside him.

Abruptly the steady, reliable hum on Kelly's right since the beginning of the flight, was broken as the engine sputtered briefly, came back to life for about a minute, sputtered again, and then went silent. Kelly was shocked at how quickly everything was happening. So much for an uneventful day, he said to himself as he unfastened his seat belt and headed for the cockpit. Five minutes later, the left engine coughed and the sequence was repeated—sputtering, power restored, another sputter—and then the left engine went silent too. Kelly was crouched behind the pilot in the cockpit. If something could be done to help, he was there to do it. His fate was tied to the pilot, who he knew was overwhelmed without a co-pilot.

The sequence of events had initially unfolded slowly, but these additional minutes they had been given weren't offering any solution. The outcome was as certain as a rising tide. Both the pilot and Kelly seemed to know it instinctively, but they remained intensely focused on the possibility that there was a way out. But no level of troubleshooting skill was going to alter the outcome for an aircraft without working engines at 20,000 feet.

The pilot had first feathered both propellers to reduce drag and increase the distance they might be able to glide. Then he had begun working methodically through a series of checklists to discover the source of the trouble. The normal procedures to restart the engines were not working. The pilot began to consider the possibility that he may not be able to bring the engines back to life. Kelly saw only a hint of tension in the actions and voice of the pilot.

"I don't want to get in the way but what can I do to help?" Kelly said simply.

The pilot motioned to a clipboard with a printed aviation map attached on the seat to the right of him.

"Grab that map and start looking for any towns or airfields from this point," he said, placing his finger on a mountainous area. "Look for any symbols, black squares or rectangles. Look from about one foot out from that spot. There might be a remote airfield down there that we can glide to."

Kelly grabbed the map and immediately began scouring it for anything that resembled a building, airfield or even a road.

"Nothing so far," he said after a minute.

The pilot pitched the nose down slightly, began a slow turn to the west and pushed the button on his microphone to call air traffic control.

"Salt Lake Center, this is November Lima 102. We're declaring an emergency. We've lost power in both engines. We're looking for the nearest airfield."

The air traffic controller came on the radio three seconds later. He confirmed the emergency and told the pilot that the nearest airport was Elk Valley, about 70 miles to the north.

The pilot released the microphone button and glanced back at Kelly. "We're not going to make that. Even with this tailwind pushing us our glide won't get us that far. What's between here and Elk Valley?"

Kelly had discarded the aviation map. He crouched with an atlas of the western U.S that he had pulled from his rucksack.

"Beyond the high peaks I don't see anything but forest, a few lakes and what looks like a couple of logging roads," he said.

Both men looked at the altimeter. And then, knowing they had no choice, they began scouring the mountains below them.

The terrain below was now more defined—the physical features of the ridges and drainages no longer had the abstract beauty of a distant, scrolling landscape but more like terrain they knew when on the ground hiking. They were descending at a rate that was unmistakable and alarming. They were both silent, but thinking the same thing: the high mountain snowfields were the only option for them.

The pilot completed another shallow turn to get a better look at the snowfields. He was trying to lose as little altitude as possible. He called the air traffic control center to update them on their altitude and then consulted with Kelly on the snow fields. The clock had ticked 15 minutes away and their altitude had been reduced proportionally. They looked down at rocky ledges, drainages with running water, and steep mountain faces.

"We're already at sixteen thousand feet," the pilot said aloud, but seemingly to himself. Kelly knew from the map some of the peaks below them were ten thousand feet high. The pilot's actions were deliberate and measured, and intently focused as only high stress can induce. He continued his efforts to troubleshoot a solution to the lifeless engines. His body seemed in continuous movement. Tension was now an equal and synchronized partner to all his skill and training, and it occupied every nerve and muscle in his body. He felt every pitch and bump of the aircraft, heard the muted rush of the air outside as if they were flying an open cockpit bi-plane, and his eyes swept the instrument panel and the ground below rapidly but with acute accuracy. His eyes registered the hazards quickly but that wasn't difficult. Because they were everywhere.

Kelly took careful measure of the pilot and concluded that, if there was a way out of this, the man flying the plane might just have the skill to pull it off. Kelly didn't respond to the pilot's comment about their altitude. He had been checking the altimeter. He was unfamiliar with most of the gauges, but he had noticed the altimeter when he saw the pilot's eyes move to it with the start of the trouble with the second engine. Now the pilot kept glancing at the altimeter, as if he was making a silent prayer.

"Start looking for a flat, open stretch of glacier—the longer the better," he said. "It's got to be fucking long. We're going in with landing gear up so we're going to slide."

Kelly nodded. His eyes were fixed on the terrain below.

They both spotted the large snowfield at the same time, an island of snow about five miles in front of them. It was a solitary patch of white encircled by a jagged landscape of rock and ice and snow. A large rock buttress sat on the uphill side with rock-terraced gullies on both ends. Below it, the snowfield dropped away steeply for several thousand feet. From their altitude, it looked little bigger than the leaf of an aspen tree. The pilot didn't like it, but he knew this was the place he had to land.

He also knew the destruction of the plane was inevitable and that escaping injury or death for both he and Kelly would be left to chance. Nothing in his training or years of flying experience offered a blueprint for what he now had to do. He was cobbling together a plan from every skill he had assembled in the past 20 years. But he believed it was possible, with a lot of luck, to land a plane here and survive.

After five more minutes they had dropped another 1500 feet. The landscape had narrowed and the aspen leaf grew. It was now the size of a large dining table. The pilot exhaled deeply and began a steeper descent.

"You should sit in the back," he said to Kelly, nodding toward the rear of the plane. "There's no need for both of us to be up here." Kelly looked at the pilot and decided not to protest. The pilot had already returned his concentration to flying the plane.

Kelly returned to his seat in the rear of the aircraft and buckled the seatbelt. His seat was only about ten feet from the cockpit and, if he leaned to his left, he had a view through the airplane's windscreen. But if he looked out of his own window, he could only see the plane's descent toward the trees and the rocky landscape. The loss of altitude seemed to happen too quickly. They were plunging toward the earth but Kelly could not see their position in relation to the snowfield. He could do nothing now but wait. He had come close to losing his life before, but those moments had always come with terrifying suddenness. They arrived like a flash of light and were gone just as quickly. Kelly was now confronted with waiting for the violence that he knew was coming, while buckled into a seat, able to do nothing to alter any part of the outcome. The seconds ticked by slowly. He wondered what Ana was doing. He knew it would be late evening where she was in Thailand. It was not too late for her to be swimming or running on the beach. He pictured her swimming close to the beach, pulling herself through the turquoise water in strong, steady strokes, thin streams of water flowing over her tanned shoulders.

The pilot flew straight toward the rock buttress on the uphill side of the snowfield and when the plane was almost level with the trees, he banked steeply to the left. The plane dove toward the snowfield.

Kelly was lifted out of his seat slightly with the sudden nose-down pitch of the plane. He instinctively tensed and his breathing halted as his body prepared for the violent momentum and violence that he knew was coming. He braced his left arm against the seat in front of him, pushed against it, and waited for the impact. But the plane was still in the air. Kelly thought that the pilot must have somehow found a larger snowfield lower down the mountain and that he was flying to it, giving them more altitude and time. It made little sense but Kelly thought it was plausible. He bent his head and looked forward into the cockpit. Suddenly he felt a thud vibrate up through the bottom of the aircraft. He didn't really believe it; it was too gentle. They had touched the earth and now the plane was skidding and bouncing on the snow, probably very fast. But that would end soon, Kelly thought, and they would be able to crawl out of the plane, stranded, but uninjured.

But at over 100 miles an hour, the aircraft was moving so fast across the surface of the snow that the fuselage was heating the surface and turning it into a thin layer of water. The plane, instead of slowing down, was now hydroplaning, and yawing one way and then another.

The pilot saw the huge boulder appear in the windscreen but he could do nothing about it. How could he have missed spotting that from the air? he thought. Where the hell had it come from? The right wingtip skidded towards it then struck it, and a torch of red-orange sparks showered the air against the white snow. The sounds of ripping metal followed. Kelly was thrown forward and his head slammed against the seat in front of him. The noise from the grinding impacts immediately shifted in pitch and intensity. The plane was cartwheeling violently and breaking apart. I will be dead in a few seconds, Kelly thought, and it seems strange that I will die here, far from the threats I have faced in my life, in a plane crash in my own country.

He could not know how many times he tumbled or how many times he impacted something inside the plane because his world was a violent spinning theater of momentum that overwhelmed his senses. He was suspended in a grey world of terrifying emancipation. He had no decisions to make now. He could only wait for the finish.

He recognized the sudden change in light, which was startling and sudden. Then the spinning stopped as quickly as it had started and he was sitting motionless on the snowfield in brilliant sunshine, still buckled into his seat. Pieces of the aircraft lay scattered around him. He recognized the forward section of the plane resting about two hundred yards downhill. He saw one of the propellers laying silent in the snow ten feet from him, no longer attached to anything. The sun was reflected in the moisture of one of the blades. Kelly's breathing was rapid and shallow and his hands seemed unable to undo his seatbelt. He finally found the metal buckle tucked under his shirt near the outside of his left hip, and he clumsily unclipped it. The seat belt, just like the propeller, he thought, was not where it belonged. He rolled out of the seat and into the snow. Then he slowly crawled downhill to the forward section of the aircraft and what was left of the cockpit.

The pilot was slumped on his left side, still seated inside the cockpit but pinned within a tangle of aluminum and plastic components which had once been the flight deck. Kelly knew instantly that he was dead. A large gash had exposed part of his skull and his body was twisted impossibly around the wreckage. Kelly reached down and placed his index finger alongside the pilot's neck, seeking a pulse, knowing he was doing it as a sign of respect as much as to confirm what he already knew. He offered a silent vow, cast not in the veil of religion but into the mountains so the world would know in some intangible way that an act of bravery had happened in this place, on this day. The outcomes for each of them had been determined by the same rules that govern a roll of the dice in a simple game of chance. But the pilot had, to the very end, kept them in the game and given them a chance. Kelly was convinced the pilot had saved his life through the careful orchestration of all his skill in that single, final act of guiding the plane into the snowfield. The pilot had given them a chance and it felt profoundly unfair that he had died. But Kelly knew that fate didn't care about equanimity, though he still wanted to believe it was possible that awareness of the pilot's last act was now rippling across the mountains toward the cities far to the west. If people understood what had happened, he reasoned, maybe that would somehow make it easier.

Kelly examined the plane's radio and quickly determined it was useless—both the microphone and the radio panel were shattered. He gathered what useful things he could reasonably carry in his small rucksack. He found a small emergency kit with some dried food and a space blanket. He found the topographic map inside the mangled front part of the plane. He searched through a flight bag that the pilot had carried and found a tube of sunscreen, several peanut butter sandwiches, some energy bars, and a down jacket. He removed the jacket and picked up the pilot's sunglasses, which were lying intact in the snow. He put all these things into the rucksack. Then he took one final look at the wreckage, and turned away.

Chapter 5

Kelly knew from the map that a town was less than 50 miles to his west, a distance he thought he could reasonably cover in three days on a road or trail. And he had enough food to sustain himself. But there were no roads or trails to the west—just steep, high peaks that towered above a series of valleys all bordered by deep, rocky drainages. His only way out was to follow a narrow river that ran northwest for nearly 100 miles as it flowed out of the mountains and into the lower elevation of the broad valley—where scattered farms and a small town lay.

    He formulated a rough plan in his head and started walking in the direction of the river. But getting to it would mean descending several thousand feet lower. His body was still flush with adrenaline from the crash but his energy began to fade when he considered what lay in front of him—a steep descent then miles of trudging along the river bottom, where he knew the brush and trees would make progress difficult and slow.

He walked across the snowfield to the edge of a large basin of snow that ran downhill toward a thick forest. He stared for a long time at the valley below and the distant mountains—trying to create a visual map of the landscape in his mind. He noted how the valley led to a range of jagged peaks to the east before twisting its way north and west. One of the peaks was striking in the way it reached toward the sky. It held a broad basin or cirque a few thousand feet below a sheer, knife-blade summit. There was something about the peak that seemed familiar to Kelly but he dismissed any notion that he knew it. He had climbed in these mountains as a teenager but he knew remote alpine peaks can all take on the same austere form and beauty.

The air was calm and the sun was high. It warmed his skin. The sky was striking in its blue contrast to the white jagged mountain ranges. He noted the time on his watch and started down the large snowfield. He slowly disappeared into the glacier-carved basin, becoming smaller and smaller against the expanse of snow.

He had been able to move quickly in the higher terrain of the snowfield, often sliding on the heels of his boots in short runs along the soft snow. But once in the forest he found himself struggling over downed trees and through thick brush. In some places it took him close to an hour to cover one mile.

He covered 10 miles before deciding to camp for the night. At times he had been able to follow game trails and old avalanche chutes, making travel slightly easier. But moving continuously over uneven terrain thick with brush and downed trees had taxed him. He was aware of the danger of exhausting himself when he didn't know what lay ahead—especially with a limited supply of food. Sok when he came to a small clearing near a creek, he dropped his rucksack and began to gather fir bows for a bed. He would sleep here for the night.

Kelly awoke to the sounds of birds flying in and out of the nearby trees. The light of the early-morning sun was spilling through the gaps in the high peaks to the east. He had slept fitfully due to the cold. During the night he had woken frequently. Then he had stood and done squats and pushups for a few minutes until he was warm enough to lie down and try to sleep again.

He studied the map closely. He knew the approximate location of the crash site and found what he thought was likely to be the broad snowfield he had just descended. He marked his location with a pen he had found in the emergency kit, and another location downriver that he hoped to make by late afternoon. He would follow the river and its meanderings, sweeping him north and eventually west, occasionally between the high peaks he had seen from the snowfield. He knew that no matter the route he traced on the map, his travel would be dictated by the unexpected meandering of the river and the game trails that allowed him to move quickly through the forest and avoid the steep slopes of the many creeks that emptied into the valley bottom. He hoped to travel 15 miles today. He ate one of the peanut butter sandwiches, packed his rucksack, filled his two water bottles, and then bent down to take a final drink from the cold creek water.

Kelly was not without worry about his circumstances. He knew he had to make the right choices and remain uninjured to get out of the mountains. But he also believed that what lay in front of him was nothing extraordinary. The distance to civilization was a 2-3 day walk, depending on what obstacles he might encounter. He had enough food for that, and he would be travelling continuously along creeks and a river, so he would always have water. The nighttime temperatures were warmer in the valley bottoms—mostly mid to low 40s. Uncomfortable for sleeping but not dangerous. All he had to do was simply follow the river until it made its final turn west toward the valley's broad expanse and reach the ranchland that marked civilization. He knew he would get hungry and be cold and sleep-deprived—the nights would be long. But the days would go quickly. It wouldn't always be comfortable, he knew, but there was nothing extraordinary about what lay ahead of him, or so he thought.

※ ※ ※

Chapter 6

He took one last look at the stamped-down grass where he had slept. Morning dew clung to the young blades and Kelly shivered slightly looking at it. He wondered briefly if another human had ever slept here, or even walked across this ground. Then he turned, confidently jumped across the small stream and entered the forest, comforted by his plan and the promise that he could move quickly in the mountains.

After a few minutes, he fell in with the rhythm of the forest and began moving efficiently through the brush, finding the open paths and avoiding slopes that might lead to small streams with heavy thickets. He descended steep slopes in long bounds where there were places free of obstacles. The movement energized and warmed him. He felt good; and his confidence grew from the progress he was making. Still, the lingering image of the plane laying broken in the snow and the lifeless body of the pilot was constantly on his mind. He had walked away from the plane crash and left the pilot behind. He knew it was the only thing he could have done, but the knowledge that he had abandoned the pilot haunted his thoughts.

By mid-afternoon, Kelly had travelled three miles. He had walked through thick brush, along game trails and across open meadows when he was lucky enough to find them adjacent to the creek banks. Finally, he made it down to the main river at the bottom of the canyon. The river would be his way home and he was relieved to reach it without a mishap.

But as Kelly began walking downriver, the terrain became harder to discern, and less predictable. He quickly came to his first major obstacle. The flat ground near the river, that had previously made travel relatively easy, began to give way to increasingly steep canyon walls. The river was also narrowing, becoming faster and more violent as it flowed through the constricted channel. It announced this new peril with a dull roar. Kelly could not see more than a quarter mile ahead and on the hillside above him the view consisted mostly of scattered cliff bands. He knew they would be dangerous to climb and could lead to even steeper terrain.

He took out his map and saw the narrow canyon in front of him matching the map's ever tightening contour lines. The terrain on his side of the river was about to turn vertical further downstream, according to the map. If he tried to climb uphill above the cliff bands, he would be moving over steep and broken rocky ground for a mile or more. The way ahead was obvious—he would need to cross to the other side of the river, where the map showed more gentle hillsides.

He put away the map and made his way back upstream, scanning the distant terrain as he went for any place where the water widened and slowed. The river itself, Kelly knew, would be dangerous to ford in its current state. It was cold and deep, and rushing and high with melting spring snow. He held out hope that he might find a wide spot where the river branched apart enough to allow him to walk across it in sections, but after a half mile, he realized he would find no such place. The river remained deep from bank to bank. He decided to hope for a random stroke of luck—a fallen tree that might span the water. He had seen several trees that had fallen into it, but none had been long enough to reach the opposite bank, their trunks anchored deep in the punishing white rapids.

Kelly came around a sharp bend in the river where the banks narrowed and constricted the surging water. His boots were wet now and his toes felt damp and cold. He reminded himself that he should dry his socks soon, or at least wring them of water, before going too much farther. He still felt strong and had no hunger, but he knew that was because he had kept moving.

In front of him, he noticed slide alder, growing thick and spindly. It began to menace him. He had to fight through narrow gaps in the brush by pulling, bending and pushing branches while trying to keep his balance and move upstream. His hands became covered in green residue from the alder, and blood from a few minor cuts. He decided to wash his hands and face in the river. The cold water would feel good on his skin.

The fast-moving river was beneath him now and throwing a tremendous volume of water through the channel. Kelly could hear large rocks tumbling and colliding as they were sent bouncing downstream along the river bottom, invisible beneath the rising and churning surface. Being so close to the water made him uneasy and he moved quickly away, back through the slide alder.

He continued through it, his movements sharpened by the now familiar task of negotiating the thick, rubbery branches. Then his left foot fell through a layer of hollow grass and he crashed forward. Even as he fell, he felt the panic rise sharply in his chest at the sensation of being pulled toward the water. His right hand instinctively grasped the trunk of a branch, slowing his crash into the grass. Lying flat against the damp soil, he could feel his heart beating. He stayed there for a few seconds, then slowly stood and took a deep breath.

As he regained his footing, he cursed the alder's seeming determination to slow him, or possibly kill him, and warned himself again about the dangers of getting hurt. He knew what even a sprained ankle could mean. Then he brushed off the dark mud that had caked on his pants from his fall and looked upstream along the near bank to see his path ahead. Then his eyes caught something he didn't expect – a movement on the opposite side of the river.

※ ※ ※

It was fragmented, obscured by the branches, but he could see that something was definitely moving near the bank, and it was not a branch in the wind. Then he noticed the large tree spanning the river. Whatever Kelly had seen had just crossed the river using the tree as a footbridge, and was now moving through the brush on the other side. The shape offered him one more shadowy flash and then quickly disappeared into the forest. He thought it had probably been a black bear. He had seen them use trees before to cross creeks and rivers. That was the only explanation that made any sense to him. He had scoured the map many times over the last 24 hours. He was deep in remote and rugged mountains with no roads or trails within at least 20 miles. A bear would make sense. But there was something in the way it moved that concerned him. He made a mental note to stay alert as he continued on his way.

He turned his attention back to the river. The massive tree, nearly three feet wide, had fallen perpendicular to the flow of the water and had made a perfect bridge, easily reaching the other side. After five more minutes of struggling through the slide alder, Kelly reached the tree. He jumped up onto the trunk resting on the near shore and tested it, finding his balance, his feet feeling for a secure perch.

Kelly started across walking quickly but deliberately along the top of the massive tree with his gaze fixed on the far bank and avoiding as much as he could the disorienting churn of the water below. But he hesitated when he came to a large branch that extended up in his path, blocking his way. His eyes inadvertently caught the moving water below. The distraction threw him off balance and he felt gravity pull him sideways. He tensed anxiously. He could feel his breathing halt but he shifted his gaze toward the far bank and the branches of a small bush. He calculated that it was within reach should he lose his footing and have to lunge for the branches. He took a breath and inched his way along the top of the tree, his boots sliding across the bark. When he was four feet from the bank he jumped, landing softly in a sandy section of the shore, the river lapping at his boots.

Kelly dropped his rucksack and lowered his right knee to the ground. He swung his gaze in a wide arc and remained still for several minutes, listening and watching. Then he pulled out his map and saw that the terrain ahead would take him up a gentle hill above a steep cliff. After that he could drop down into more gentle ground on the far side, and eventually into flat, open areas that ran adjacent to the river for several miles. Beyond that, the landscape would gradually open to a broad valley, where he believed scattered farms could be found.

But first Kelly needed to dry off and eat something. He removed his boots and socks and wrung out the latter. Then he pulled out one of the peanut butter sandwiches and took two bites. Of course, the brief taste would only make him more hungry, but he knew he had to put fuel in his body. He wrapped the rest of the sandwich up reluctantly and placed it inside his pack.

He shouldered his rucksack and began moving on through the trees and up the hill in a long traverse. The forest was littered with broken branches, pine needles and pinecones, but it was mostly free of brush. Kelly felt an urgency to return to civilization and tell people about the crash. But he knew he had to be careful. While his path out of the mountains was relatively direct now that he was next to the river, he knew that the mountains had a way of surprising you. For that reason, he moved slowly, to pace himself.

He reached the summit of the hill after 20 minutes. It was bare of trees or brush and offered an unobstructed view of the river below and the open plains to the west, where the river eventually led. Kelly dropped his rucksack. He would camp here for the night.

Chapter 7

The night air was warmer here than it had been in the upper mountains and Kelly hoped to sleep in long stretches. He wrapped himself tightly in the emergency blanket and was able to tunnel his body under a layer of fir boughs that he had gathered before nightfall. They provided additional warmth, and also concealed him among the dark silhouette of several small trees. It was an old habit, to remain hidden, but he remembered what he had seen crossing the river.

Above him the last fading light revealed the trees as looming figures, swaying slightly in the evening breeze. He pulled the emergency blanket closer and his mind went back to the crash site and the pilot. He wondered where he had grown up, if he had played sports in school, what he did on the weekends, if he had children and a wife. Then Kelly closed his eyes and drifted off to sleep, the sound of the river below growing softer and more distant.

※ ※ ※

He was up and packing his things into the rucksack as the sun touched the upper branches of the forest's towering fir trees. He felt good; rested and eager to make progress toward civilization, to all its comforts—a warm bed, a hot shower and all the food he wanted. But most of all he was anxious to be back among other people so that he could tell them what had happened. His family and friends would be worried about him – it was now over a day since the plane had crashed. He knew the military and local authorities would have set in motion the normal procedures for responding to a missing aircraft. Kelly wondered if they had located the crash site. He hadn't seen any aircraft flying overhead so he assumed whatever the authorities knew, they probably had not been able to detect an emergency signal and pinpoint the high basin where the pilot had maneuvered the plane. For Kelly, that didn't matter. He had already decided the only way out of the mountains was on foot. Mostly, his urgency centered around the pilot's family. He felt it as a profound responsibility, to tell them what had happened.

Less cautious now that he was away from the thick brush and the fast-moving river, Kelly set out on a downhill stretch of mostly open forest that lay in front of him. He moved easily, bounding over fallen trees and through open glades. He ran in the places where gravity gave him the advantage, weaving among the scattered timber as he aimed back to the river in a long downhill descent, his rucksack rising and slapping against his lower back. His body grew warm and became stronger as he moved. He was again finding harmony with the terrain.

He came to a flat area that surrounded the river, an open flood plain that reached as far as he could see. The travelling from here would be easier now that he was past the steep canyon. He stopped briefly, pulled out his map, and found the widely spaced topographic lines showing a gradual descent. He was hopeful that he might cover 30 miles today if there were no setbacks. He set off again and moved quickly for the first five miles, stopping only to check his map once and drink from the river. He crossed several small tributary streams that ran out of the mountains to his right. The streams were flush with snow-melt and the water formed narrow, rocky channels that were only two to three feet wide. Most of these, Kelly easily jumped over. Then he came to a broad meadow which had a small stream running through its middle, the water moving fast and urgently to join the river, which was fed by the numerous mountain streams and had now gained considerable energy.

The small stream in front of Kelly was bordered by dense stands of willows that gave way to a narrow gap that offered an easy way across the sliver of water. Kelly instinctively moved through the tall grass toward the gap. He reached the near bank and was planting his foot to spring across in one motion when something unusual caught his eye. Then he froze. Something red, bright and shiny, hung in the willows. It was a red ribbon and so out of place that he couldn't help but stare at it. The thin strand of fabric was about ten inches long and suspended from a branch on the other side of the stream. It drifted brightly in the light breeze running through the willows.

Kelly cast his gaze left and right but there was nothing that offered a clue to its origin. He jumped across the stream and gently lifted the ribbon off the branch. His mind ran through all the possibilities but nothing offered a reasonable explanation for how a ribbon would end up deep in the mountains, far from civilization, unless it had been carried here by someone. He held it up in the light of the sun; it was not faded or weathered. Even after a week, the elements would have altered its shine and texture, he knew. He thought it could only have been on the branch for a day or two, though he couldn't reconcile in his mind how it had got there. But as puzzling as it was, the origin of the ribbon was not what mattered most to him right now.

He put the ribbon in his pocket and continued across the meadow. He followed game trails through the open areas of the flood plain for another ten miles before stopping to eat half of one of the remaining sandwiches in his rucksack. It was the only thing he would eat today other than a handful of almonds he planned to have for dinner. He sat with his back against a large fir tree and his legs outstretched in front of him, perched on a small knoll overlooking the river. The spring sun was still high and he could feel its pulsing heat on his skin. The rushing river reminded him that life in the mountains was easier now than it would have been two months ago. The new life of spring was all around him, showing itself in the green shoots of grass and new buds of the Sitka alder and willow.

Kelly pulled the ribbon from his pocket and examined it. There was nothing unique about it except for the fact that it had ended up here. *That* was the very definition of unique, he thought. He had not seen any other sign of humans—trails, footprints, or campsites since he had left the aircraft wreckage. Kelly wondered if the ribbon had been carried into the sky attached to a party balloon, or if it had simply been carried here on thermal currents that were strong enough to take it over the highest peaks into the cooler mountain air where it fell out of the sky. He had seen party balloons in the mountains before, or what was left of them. He had noticed them hanging high up in branches in the most remote and inhospitable places—their final resting places after traveling with the strong summer thermal currents thousands of feet above the mountains. But he hadn't seen any evidence of a balloon when he found the ribbon. He wondered about its journey to get to this place so far from its origin. It was not unlike his own journey, he thought. He would never know the ribbon's story and it only proved to him that some things were an odd mix of design and chance, so many things hitched to others that were always evolving—and none of it explainable. He put the ribbon back in his pocket.

Kelly had felt the acute pangs of hunger the day before but over the last 24 hours his body had begun adjusting to just a few hundred calories a day. He knew such a small amount of food would not sustain him for long and the impacts of hunger on his body and mind would start to accumulate each day. But, for now, he had found a rhythm moving alongside the river, following its meandering curves as they both made their journey out of the mountains. His body was worn and weather beaten by the endless miles of negotiating obstacles, and the occasional battles with thick brush, but Kelly felt immersed in this world now. He was not in a battle against it or weakened by it. He had moved faster today and found a pace that he felt he could sustain for at least another day. He looked at his map and estimated that he could make it into the valley, reaching one of the forest roads that accessed the mountains by the end of tomorrow. It would be a long day, but he knew it was possible if things went well. For now, he would rest for 20 minutes before continuing on until just before sunset. He removed his shirt and let the sun's rays warm his skin. He moved away from the tree and propped his rucksack behind his head, stretching out in the foot-tall grass on the flat ground and closing his eyes. His mind quickly found a rhythm with the sound of the river and its loud rush of power and balance. He was soon lost in a state of blissful half sleep.

A familiar dream came to Kelly, fragments of which he felt he had experienced for most of his life. But in reality he had only been having the dream in the last ten years. Most of the time he could not make out any details after waking; he didn't know the people or the place. The pieces seemed always connected in random ways to other events in his life—some of which he recognized—but any real meaning eluded him. This time, however, the images were vivid and coherent, the story was playing out in every corner of his unconscious mind, and none of it felt like a dream.

He had been high up in the mountains, well above the forest below, alone, and descending a steep, late spring snowfield. The sky was such a brilliant blue that it was hard to imagine it could ever be dangerous. The air still. It was his 22nd birthday. And he was running down the snowfield, bounding several feet with each step, letting his climbing boots sink a few inches into the soft, sun-soaked snow before pushing off again in the joyous freedom of momentary weightlessness. He let gravity carry him down the expansive high mountain cirque in a celebration of movement and natural wonder. The dream then shifted and he was on a snow bank and launching himself across a mountain stream from the high bank to reach the other side, suspended in mid-air over the deep recess of the creek and the rocks below, reaching for the snow bank on the far side of the creek and toward the bright red jacket directly in front of him.

He was reaching, and trying to run, still in the air, reaching for a young girl who was wearing the red jacket.

He woke suddenly, his skin still warm in the bright sun. The river was still rushing by in a peaceful chorus as the light breeze danced through the aspens. But Kelly was anxious, his breathing was shallow as he sat up in the grass.

The dream's images had been so powerful that his conscious mind was still partly held in their world, even as he focused his attention on his watch. He'd been asleep for an hour. He needed to get moving.

He gathered his jacket and rucksack, checked his map and began walking through the meadow that ran next to the river. He found a faint game trail, but in his mind was a sensation of the snowfield and weightlessness, and an image of the brightest red he had ever seen.

The images from the dream were still with him as he moved through the last section of the meadow and saw that he had to ascend an open hillside that climbed up three hundred feet, where there was a dramatic change in the topography.

The river had taken a sharp left turn and was now heading slightly north into a canyon-like escarpment. The hill in front of Kelly would finally get him above the canyon and would probably be high enough to view the broad valley which his map told him would lead him out of the mountains to the west. It took him 20 minutes to crest the top of the hill. He felt fatigue in his muscles for the first time. His legs were heavy and his body had started resisting the continued effort.

Kelly stopped and rested both arms on his uphill leg, allowing himself a few minutes to recover. His grey pants displayed dried dirt from his occasional falls and tumbles over the last two days. He had removed his jacket and wore a long-sleeved black nylon shirt that was damp with sweat. His expression was nevertheless relaxed and comfortable, his mind focused on moving ahead.

Kelly continued through a flat, open area surrounded by large, old-growth fir trees that towered overhead, reaching, it seemed, for the high peaks upslope to the east. Kelly dropped his rucksack in the soft pine needles of the forest floor. He took his water bottle from the pack and walked to the edge of the hill on its western end and took in the view toward the valley, which extended to a distant range of mountains on the far side. For the first time, he was able to make out the shapes of scattered farmhouses and a single long road that ran from it into the mountains. He could make it there by tomorrow, he thought. Then he looked to the east toward the towering peaks. He examined the ridgelines and the summits and the narrow couloirs that sharply dropped away from their jagged summits. The most prominent couloir gave way to a broad and steep snowfield. It looked like it was at least a half mile long. He traced the edges of it where it met the sections of rock and visualized the lower areas that were obscured by trees and rock bands. He stood there, staring, for several minutes, his mind seeing the features of the mountains and how a climber might approach them—seeking out the lines to take to the summit. It was a practice that evolved from the countless hours he had spent seeking out high peaks when climbing—sometimes reaching the top, sometimes never getting close for all kinds of reasons.

He'd always been drawn to mountains and when he was old enough, he had committed several years of his youth to climbing them. But as Kelly analyzed the rock and snow of the peaks above the forest, his subconscious mind was recalling something else. This train of thought continued as he slowly turned and walked back to his rucksack. Kelly didn't know why, but after a few steps he stopped suddenly and turned around. A little farther uphill from where he had stood to look at the mountains was a large boulder, about twelve feet high. It was majestic and beautiful but completely out of place, sitting conspicuously in the middle of the old growth forest. The north side of it was mostly covered in moss. The south end had several ledges and prominent cracks that ran vertically to its top. Kelly thought it was strange he hadn't noticed it before. The view will be slightly better from up there, he thought. He began walking toward it.

Kelly examined the rock briefly before he scrambled up it in a series of graceful movements, his hands finding leverage in its deep cracks. His final move was a long reach for the sloping top where his fingers found a thin, horizontal ridge. It offered a perfect hold. He pushed off from his uphill leg and pulled himself up with both arms, and as he cleared the crest of the granite, he thought his eyes were tricking him. He made the final step to the top and crouched down next to the ridge. He felt startled and unsettled as he realized it was real, but he quickly picked it up. In his hand was another thin piece of ribbon, about a foot long. Once again, it was not weather-beaten or faded. And once again, it was red.

He put the ribbon in his pocket with the first piece, and scrambled back down the boulder. He would try to make sense of it later, he decided. For now, he needed to make a place to stay the night, a place that might allow an hour of sleep, or hopefully more, before the cold rousted him.

The last of the sun spread along the jagged rock spires and patchy snow fields of the high peaks in a shifting blend of red and pink. Kelly lay watching it all with his back against his rucksack. He had found enough fir bows to construct a makeshift bed that would trap some warmth from his body during the night. He watched the colors in the sky go from fire red to a fading pink and purple glow. They ran across the top of the entire mountain range, all the way, Kelly imagined, to the Pacific Ocean.

He reached into his pocket and ran his thumb and forefinger along the flat, smooth texture of the ribbon—the most recent one—that he had found on the boulder. He had found it because it was so prominent and out of place in the forest, and it offered a spectacular vantage point to survey the terrain below. Maybe someone else had stood there for the same reason. He thought about that and wondered if there was someone else in the forest leaving no trail but following the same terrain as him. He thought it would be incredibly unlikely but it was still possible, he knew.

As the last colors from the setting sun faded above the peaks, Kelly was already drifting off to sleep.

He slept for 30 minutes before the cold woke him. He knew it wouldn't help rest his legs, but after waking for a second time, Kelly got up and began doing squats and pushups to warm his body. He would do 20 pushups and 20 squats and lay down again, curling into a tight ball under the fir bows and his emergency blanket to trap as much of his body heat as possible. He repeated this cycle throughout the night—sleep, shivering and exercise, over and over again. When the sun finally peaked over the eastern skyline, he was happy to get moving once more, images of a warm bed and hot food now prevalent in his thoughts.

After an hour of moving, most of it spent descending the small hill on which he had camped and travelling easily along the river once again, he finally allowed the stress of finding his way out of the mountains to move to the back of his mind. Not gone, but less pressing. For the first time since the crash, he permitted himself the comfort of believing that the primary challenges were now behind him. The valley was about ten miles away according to his map and when he came to elevated points that allowed a view he could see the valley broaden and he was able to identify more features of civilization—the farm roads that ran straight for several miles and what he thought was a train track. He was getting close.

But then the river entered another section of steep terrain and he had to move uphill to avoid a series of cliffs. He was now travelling in another old-growth forest with the river far below and out of sight. The day began to feel much warmer than any of the previous ones. And deep among the towering trees there was nothing even close to a breeze. His shirt was now soaked in sweat. After half a mile of climbing over and under huge old, fallen trees and squeezing his way through patches of nearly impenetrable slide alder, Kelly found a rhythm in simply moving, and he focused his mind only on that.

His life had been rootless for the most part since he had left the military. Certainly not devoid of meaning and fulfillment, as he usually had something on the horizon—a short work stint or a climbing adventure that would occupy him for a few weeks. But in other ways he fitted the definition of someone searching for stability and it was inevitable that his restlessness made happiness elusive. But here, deep in the natural world, with the security of food and shelter non-existent, he was somehow completely content and present, even with its discomforts. His mind was now a partner to his body and its movement, and he thought about nothing else. His job was to just keep moving.

And then, almost without Kelly noticing, the forest began to change. Just a few hundred feet ahead of him the dark interior was giving way to a long panel of light filtering through the thinning trees. He thought he must be approaching a steep snow-filled drainage—an avalanche chute—that ran from the high peaks to his right. He'd encountered several of them over the last two days. Soon he could see the far bank of the drainage and he knew the chute would probably be narrow and covered with snow bridges. They would be potentially difficult to cross but he was glad to finally be leaving the forest and its obstacles. He stepped from the edge of the trees and onto the soft snow, remnants of a winter avalanche, spilling out from a deeper gully just ahead of Kelly . His foot sank and almost immediately slipped and he caught himself with his arm, bracing it against the snow but sinking up to his elbow. He stood up and kicked two solid steps into the snow with his boots. He took a deep breath. His body was adjusting to the new element under his feet. He reminded himself to be careful. In front of him was a rushing stream strewn fueled by the melted snow from the winter's avalanches. Kelly instinctively looked up toward the high peaks and saw that the narrow chute expanded quickly above the tree line into a broad bowl. He was standing near the terminus of a stream flush with spring snow-melt that was crashing its way down the mountain in a loud roar of energy. Some of the water was falling onto the large boulders next to the stream and sending sheets of cool spray into the air, creating rising curtains of mist. Kelly felt the cold exhilaration from the evaporating showers on his face and arms and it energized him after hours battling through the heat of the forest. The roar of the rushing creek erased all other sounds. Kelly realized he was slightly disoriented by the sound and the radical change in scenery and the unstable snow under his feet—but he was eager to gather some cold water from the stream before finding a place to cross. He stepped forward onto the snow. And then he froze.

When he thought back on the moment the next day, Kelly realized he had only seen her eyes. And even when it happened, he didn't comprehend that her gaze and his were locked on each other for only a second. It seemed like several minutes, as they both searched for the clues that were elusive but also real. The sound of the stream was lost somewhere in Kelly' consciousness. The world had changed somehow.

Chapter 8

She was seated on a large boulder about 20 feet up from the far bank of the stream. She moved her head only slightly to gaze upslope, following the line of the creek to the high mountain peaks, strands of her long, light brown hair covering her face; her hair damp from the light showers of water sent up from the creek as it crashed on the rocks. Her eyes the color of a blue-green glacier. Her body was steady and poised as she scanned the terrain above, while still aware of Kelly's presence. Kelly followed her gaze up the drainage and then they both looked at each other again. Kelly raised his arm and waved. She waved back. He scanned the creek for a way across and saw a car-sized snow bridge about 30 feet uphill.

He quickly made his way up to it. He tested it and moved to step to the middle but then stopped and looked down the far side of the boulder-strewn stream bank to see if the girl was still there. He had experienced hallucinations from sleep deprivation before and if that was what had just happened to him, he thought, it would explain a lot. It would explain everything. But she was still there, watching him. He stepped to the middle of the snow bridge, pushed off and jumped to the far side of the stream. Then he made his way up to the girl, hopping from one large boulder to another. She sat watching him intently. Kelly found a large boulder a few feet up hill from her, close enough so she could hear him over the roaring stream, and dropped his rucksack. He sat down on the rock. He saw a rucksack resting upright on the rocks next to the girl, leaving against the boulder she was sitting on. A red jacket was strapped to the outside.

"I haven't seen anyone for three days," he said. "Where is the rest of your family?"

The girl looked at Kelly and smiled. "I'm a family of one," she said.

"You're up here by yourself?"

"Yes."

Kelly had dismissed his intuition when he had seen her from the other side of the creek. Mostly because it made no sense. It just wasn't possible. But now, hearing her voice and seeing how she sat on the rock, like she belonged there, he knew he had been right. It was unmistakable instinct coming from the depth of his memory: he knew this girl.

"But how…"

"I'm 14," she said, sparing Kelly the rest of his question.

"But you're in the middle of nowhere," he said.

"So are you."

"But I was in a plane crash. I'm walking out of the mountains," Kelly said.

"I'm walking into the mountains," the girl said. "I came from there." She pointed up the canyon toward the headwaters of the river that Kelly had been following.

Kelly looked at her, his mind trying to piece together his past and this girl and how she had been able to find her way so far from the nearest town through terrain that was so steep and remote travel would be more than difficult, even on a trail.

A dark blue, long-sleeved nylon shirt was hanging loosely off her shoulders and the scuffed but sturdy leather hiking boots on her feet looked like they were part of this landscape of snow and rock. A pair of dark sunglasses hung around her neck, partially hidden by her wavy long hair. Laying against the rock next to her was a pair of trekking poles. Her rucksack was packed to the top and had a sleeping pad strapped neatly to the outside. Her light blue nylon pants were rolled up to just above her knees and her tanned legs were splattered with dried mud. She wore a wool, dark grey beanie, the brim just touching her eyebrows.

"Do you have a map and food?" Kelly asked.

"Of course, I have food. I don't have a map."

"I'm sorry," Kelly said, "but how you got here is really confusing to me."

"You're the one who got here in a plane crash," she answered.

Kelly laughed softly. "Okay, fair enough," he said. "What's your name?"

"Ella."

"That's a good name for a strong girl who travels in the mountains by herself," Kelly said, as he dug into his rucksack and found one of the remaining energy bars he had recovered from the airplane. He reached out his arm and handed it to her.

She looked at the yellow wrapper. "It's lemon flavored," she said smiling. "Thank you."

Ella sat eating with her eyes fixed on Kelly. "Did you get hurt when the plane crashed?" she asked after a few minutes.

"No, I'm OK," Kelly said. "But the pilot didn't make it."

"He died?" Ella asked.

"Yes."

"I'm sorry."

Kelly looked at her and smiled. He was struck by her unshakable sense of calm. Her eyes were still fixed on him. Kelly searched his memory. Ella. He should remember her. Maybe she played on the youth soccer team he had helped coach when he was on a three-month training assignment in northwest Montana five years ago.

He threw that idea out to himself, though he knew it was pedestrian and useless. He remembered those kids well. He would not have forgotten Ella. But he knew his dreams over the last several years had been extraordinarily real at times, so much so that the events of his life and the visions that unfolded at night had somehow become intertwined. It was unsettling to Kelly but he wondered if he knew Ella from one of those dreams.

"Where was the pilot from?" she asked.

"I don't know," Kelly said. "I didn't really know him."

"But people will miss him, won't they?" Ella said.

"I'm sure people will miss him very much," Kelly said. "He was a very brave man."

"I wonder if we ever stop missing people?"

Kelly saw the clarity and curiosity of the question in her eyes.

"I don't know," he said. "Maybe if we are generous toward them when they are with us, then we don't miss them so much."

"Maybe it's better to never stop missing them completely," Ella said.

Kelly looked at her and nodded. "It probably is better"

Kelly reached into his rucksack and pulled out his water bottle.

"Do you have a water bottle that needs filling?" he asked her.

She pulled a bottle from the side pocket of her pack and handed it to him. He moved over the large boulders to the creek and held the bottles one at a time in a stream of water that surged over the rocks. The water was icy cold on Kelly's hand and forearm as he held the bottles tightly to keep the water from ripping them from his grasp. Then he sealed them with their caps and moved back to where Ella was sitting.

He handed her the bottle. "This should be enough for this evening but we can fill them again in the morning before we leave," he said. "The river will be near us for most of the way out."

Ella looked at him with a puzzled expression.

"You're not going that way?" Kelly asked.

Ella shook her head.

"I'm kind of afraid to ask this," Kelly said after a few seconds, "but where are you going?"

Ella looked at him warmly, and then her eyes moved to the creek and its tumbling water, and then traced the path of the stream upslope to the high peaks. "Up there," she said.

"That's what I thought," Kelly said. "I have to get to the valley as soon as possible."

"I understand," Ella said.

"You can come with me," Kelly said.

Ella remained silent; her gaze fixed on Kelly.

"You won't come with me?" Kelly said finally.

"No."

"Climbing up there could be difficult," Kelly said, setting his eyes on the upper snowfield above them.

"I am bringing my parents back to the place they loved the most," Ella said.

Before Kelly had time to consider what Ella had just said, she added, "You can come with me."

Kelly could neither say yes or no to that question. He needed time to consider everything that had just happened since he had first seen Ella from the other side of the creek.

"Are you camping here tonight," Kelly asked.

"Yes, I have a flat spot up there a little way, at the edge of the boulders" Ella said, gesturing to a small stand of trees behind her. "You should camp up there, too," she said. "It's a nice spot and we have the creek right here for water."

"Thank you," Kelly said. "I'll camp here with you then."

As he followed Ella up to the camp spot Kelly could only think about which direction he would be traveling in the morning. The obligation he felt to the pilot had not left him but he knew that Ella could get hurt while climbing alone and if that happened there would be no one to help her. He told himself she was strong and capable and would likely be ok, as she had already traveled this far on her own. But he remembered his own mishaps in the mountains when he was younger and that was something he could not push aside easily. He knew the constant dangers of the mountains, especially in the higher alpine areas that harbored rockfall and collapsing snow fields.

※ ※ ※

Kelly was still struggling with the question of what direction he would be travelling in the morning as he made his way through the heavy brush west of where he had briefly left Ella to look for more food. And while there was still no resolution to the question, as he finally found a way across the river on a series of connecting logs in a wide, braided spot of the channel, his conscience had already pointed him to the direction he would take. Ella was alive. Her travel would likely be less dangerous if Kelly joined her. He could do nothing for the pilot.

But he knew with certainty that extra food was something that would benefit them both regardless of what direction Kelly would travel in the morning. And so it was that he found himself once again stepping ever so carefully across a large tree that lay on its side above a raging torrent of the ice-cold river, his eyes fixed on the far bank. He leapt for it and landed in the soft grass with a victorious feeling. But he quickly reminded himself he would have to return across the same log so kept any sense of celebration for later.

He pulled his map from his pants' cargo pocket and located the black-inked symbol indicating a small structure—the map's legend even went so far as giving it the name "remote cabin." It might actually be there, and if they were lucky, it might actually have food, Kelly had thought when he had checked the map while sitting with Ella an hour earlier at their camp spot. He knew these maps often didn't match what was on the ground when it came to things like human-built structures deep in the mountains where they can burn down, be torn down or simply fall apart from decay. But he still had three hours of daylight. He had to try.

He put the map back in his pocket and began walking downriver toward the black symbol which on the map was directly in the middle of widely spaced topographic lines. It was an elevated, bench area on the landscape that for, whatever reason, had escaped the scouring and eroding effect of the river over millions of years. If he was in the right spot, he would come across the cabin in half a mile.

After 20 minutes, Kelly saw the ground ahead of him begin to push upward into a thinly covered slope of large pine trees and a few islands of shrubs. Several large, granite boulders, some as high as a single-story building, were scattered along the hillside, resting permanently in the soft layer of decaying branches and pine needles. He crossed a trickle of a stream and left the last section of heavy brush. The ground in front of him rose upward as he got closer. The day's heat was mostly gone now and he put on his light jacket as he climbed through the shaded forest and over the top of the hill, where he was met by a meadow. It was an unexpected find, but here it was, a long field of grass on an elevated plateau, bending in a light breeze and catching the afternoon's last golden rays. He could see to the far end, which covered about 20 acres, but as he walked another 50 feet to the interior and cast his gaze from left to right, it was obvious there was no cabin. Even the shoulder-high grass and the ground's undulations could not have hidden one. Kelly resisted the immediate tug of disappointment. He knew coming here had been a long shot. But he also knew that fate—that mysterious passenger that orchestrated the alchemy of time and place and fortune, good and bad—traveled with him unseen, but always present.

To get a better look at the meadow, and because he had already come this far, he began to walk slowly north around the meadow's perimeter, starting at its lower side to his right. It took him about five minutes before he was near the northwest corner on the upper part. He noticed that here the grass had become shorter and somewhat patchy, pocked with a few weeds. This was in sharp contrast to the tall, seamless expanse of healthy blades that he had been walking through. This area was also broken up by small pine trees and scattered rocks. There was a small mound, about five feet high, directly in front of him. He knew this spot had been altered in some way. He walked to the top of the mound and from there looked toward the forest. Nothing caught his attention but his instincts urged him onward. He scrambled down the small hill and into the trees.

Within about 100 feet, Kelly's eye was drawn to a narrow, patchy strand of dirt on the forest floor. It was only a foot wide but was mostly free of rocks and branches. It was faint but Kelly immediately recognized it as a primitive trail, most likely used by animals but maybe also humans. He quickly found its bearing and followed it with a renewed urgency, his eyes scanning the ground ten to twenty feet ahead at a time, not wanting to lose its course. Within a minute he had covered several hundred feet and entered an ancient part of the forest where the small, spindly trees had been replaced by very large, towering old ones—likely to be several hundred years old, he estimated. The trail was littered with branches that had fallen in a mosaic of random patterns that only a wild forest can create. Kelly came to a massive fallen tree that he had to climb over to stay on the trail. His feet slid gently to the ground as he lowered himself and he turned and swung his front leg over a large branch.

He was turning to get back on the trail when the sight of the cabin's roofline startled him. The effect was like the loud crack of a rifle fired in a dark, eerily quiet forest. The long, exacting line was so distinct and out of place from everything his eyes had become accustomed to over the last several days that he wasn't sure at first that it was real. He was too far away to clearly see any more of it yet, but the shape was unmistakably of human design. He stepped quickly over the branch and was almost in a slow run by the time he got to a small, sturdy cabin with a single rectangular window and a short, stubby door made from rough planks.

Kelly knew that he was deep in the middle of the forest now. He slowed to a careful walk, pausing twice to examine his surroundings. When he got to the front door, he began a slow walk around the outside of the cabin. It was made of rough timber, cut from the surrounding forest. Kelly could see that it was well taken care of, all the seams between the timbers had been recently caulked and the mountain winters had only left grey streaks on some of the planks. The roof was metal and covered with pine needles. A few fallen branches lay scattered on the hard metal surface. Kelly returned to the front door, put his hand on the latch, and pushed it down slowly. The door swung open easily, propelled by its own weight. A small wooden table stood in the center of the cabin, with a wooden bench tucked underneath. The light that spilled in from the open door illuminated a stacked pile of material in the corner. It was tucked away neatly and covered by a dark brown tarp. The walls had only two bare shelves and no cabinets.

Kelly realized this was nothing more than a simple shelter—and one not stocked for emergencies. There was most likely no food here. He sighed and walked over to the tarp. He pulled it up, expecting to find tools for maintaining the cabin, or maybe even firewood for the small wood stove that stood in another corner. But laying beneath the tarp were several brightly colored duffle bags. Kelly pulled one of them off the pile and unzipped it. A folded nylon bag, about the size of a small suitcase, a large backpack and two harnesses, lay packed together inside the duffle bag. Kelly recognized the design of the harnesses – they we made for paragliding. He searched the other duffle bag and realized he had come across a complete kit for tandem paragliding.

Kelly had flown paragliders for six years before entering the military. It had started as a way to descend from high peaks with two friends who had previously learned to fly in Europe. After one summer spent watching them fly off the mountains that the three of them had hiked or climbed, while he had to make the long walk down, Kelly had taken up the sport. For two years, it had been the focus of his life and he had travelled with his friends to Europe to chase weather and conditions suitable for long cross-country flights.

But he hadn't flown in five years and a paraglider wasn't the item he had come to the cabin in search of. He thought it seemed remarkably out of place in this remote little cabin. He packed everything back in the duffle bags and started searching a heavier canvas bag he had found inside one of the duffle bags. In one of the pack's side pockets he found six cans of tuna fish. He sighed with relief and stuffed them inside his rucksack. Then he turned and walked out of the cabin, closing the door behind him.

When he reached the meadow, he glanced at the sky. It was something he had been doing constantly since the crash. High up in the air, he saw very faint, wispy streaks of mares' tails; only two or three, but they caught his attention. He kept walking. After another twenty steps he looked up again and saw a red-tailed hawk several hundred feet above him. It tilted a wing into a strong thermal as it banked and adjusted its course, balancing on the lifting air and gently feeling the pressure and responding to it as the air carried it skyward. Kelly paused for several seconds, watching the hawk, and then turned around. He would take the paraglider with him, he decided. On his hike to the cabin, he had had several good vantage points of the high peak that Ella had gestured to from the creek. He had looked closely at the snowfields, the creek that ran down from the highest snowfield, and the bands of rock that bordered the snowfields. He believed it all could be climbed in one or two days. The simple protection of a nylon paraglider, refashioned as a tent, could offer some warmth at the very least. He didn't like the idea of taking it, it wasn't his property, and he and Ella were not in dire need of it—but something told him to go back and get it. So that's exactly what he did.

Kelly retrieved the large backpack and put the paraglider, harnesses, and other gear inside it. He did not need the two harnesses but they were light and easy to pack away and he thought he and Ella could sleep on them and be insulated from the ground.

Then he started the walk back through the forest to where he had left Ella. He was moving much faster than he had been on the trip out, mostly due to knowing the route—but also because he now felt an urgency to return to Ella, to share the good news with her. He also didn't like being separated from her. He crossed the river on the same trees, which was more difficult with the 20 pounds of gear on his back. But his feet knew the feel and the texture of its bark now and he was more confident. When he got to Ella she was sitting on one of the large boulders near the stream, the light of the day starting to fade toward dusk. She was reading *The Little Prince* by Antoine de Saint-Exupéry. She set the book on one of the flat rocks next to her when she saw Kelly approaching from the lower part of the boulder field.

"What did you find over there?" she asked.

"Several cans of tuna fish," he said as he swung the large pack off his back. "We can have some for dinner," he added, smiling. "The cans looked okay, no bulging or dents or anything but we can smell it when we open it to make sure."

"Tuna is probably the greatest thing you could have found over there, except maybe for chocolate," Ella replied.

"I also found a paraglider that we can use tonight to make a tent—it'll be warmer."

"Or we can use it to fly off the mountain."

He laughed. "Do you always think like that?"

"Like what?"

"Like really big and slightly dangerous."

"You're the one who got here by crashing a plane."

"Yes, you keep reminding me of that."

"Is that how you got here before?" she asked.

Kelly paused from pulling the paraglider from its pack. He looked at Ella and something in his memory flickered, a flash of recollection, as intense as the flinty smell of gunpowder, but it was gone as quickly as it had arrived. To his conscious mind, it was too vague but he knew intuitively something in his past had been brought forward. He shifted his feet on the boulders to get a better grip on the pack and knocked his water off the rock it was resting on. It fell between the rocks.

"Oh no, I can get it," Ella said. "My arms will fit between those rocks."

She scrambled over to Kelly and effortlessly retrieved the water bottle.

Kelly let Ella's question go. It was going to be dark soon and they needed to build a shelter out of the paraglider. He smiled at her.

"Here," she said, handing him a slice of dried mango. "You should eat this. I haven't seen you eat anything at all."

Kelly took the food from Ella's hand. "Thank you," he said.

They shared a can of tuna and ate in silence for the most part. The sound of the creek filled the air.

Kelly found a flat spot on the edge of the boulder field where a patch of heather had taken root near several stubby trees. He strung the paraglider fabric from the tops of the small trees to a large boulder and used the excess fabric to make walls, anchored to the ground by rocks he pulled from the boulder field. It was cold but Ella and Kelly slept side by side and the nylon fabric trapped enough of their body heat to make the night comfortable enough for both of them.

Chapter 9

Kelly was awakened by birds singing. They were perched on the nearby boulders, hopping from rock to rock, occasionally taking to the air to land by small pools in the creek, where they bobbed their heads to drink. The sun had barely begun to lighten the forest below and give shape to the high mountain peaks above. The sound of the creek was less noticeable now. Kelly rolled out of the nylon shelter and put his boots and jacket on. Then he hiked to a high spot slightly uphill. He wanted to see more of the terrain above their campsite. When he returned, Ella was packing things into her small rucksack. The sun was now cresting the tall mountains behind them and spilling light onto the rocky ridges above the far snowfields on the other side of the canyon.

As he was walking back down to Ella, Kelly glanced at the distant mountains and located two high peaks with a broad snowfield directly below. He knew that the crashed wreckage of the plane was resting there, the body of the pilot within it. It bothered him that he knew what had happened to the pilot but the man's family and friends still did not. Kelly had a role in that crash just by the fact that he had been in the plane, and he was tied to those events and to that spot, whether he liked it or not. He wondered what that meant, how it might alter his life. He allowed his mind to be pulled back to Ella, this peculiar young girl and her journey deep into the mountains. The sound of the crashing creek, only 100 feet from them, took hold of his thoughts. He looked intently at the rhythmic flow of the water in the creek, its relentless energy as it moved over and around the boulders in the creek. It put to rest his deliberation. He was going to climb upward with Ella.

Ella made some final adjustments to her pack and put away her water bottle. She shouldered her pack as Kelly was folding the paraglider into its nylon bag. Ella looked at him and said, "Maybe I will see you here again sometime?"

Kelly looked up, surprised to see the pack already on her back, her boots already in motion, heading across the broad expanse of large boulders stretching up to the high peaks. Tucked under the left shoulder strap of her pack was a small red ribbon.

"Wait," he said.

She found a flat area on one of the large boulders and sat on its edge. Then she gave him a quizzical look.

Kelly stuffed the rest of the paraglider into its backpack and packed his small rucksack inside. He grabbed a quarter of a sandwich from the top of the large backpack lid and stuffed it into his mouth.

"Okay," he said, smiling at Ella. "Let's go."

"You're going with me?"

"I want to see what's up there," he said, pointing to the high peaks.

"Okay, then I'll be happy to have you along as my cook and porter."

"I'll try to keep up."

Ella smiled and turned toward the mountain.

She moved steadily up through the boulder field, bounding from rock to rock, sometimes testing the more unstable looking rocks before committing her full weight to them. Kelly followed closely behind. Soon they were both moving in a rhythm, almost synchronized in their pace and placement of each step. Their thoughts became lost in their movements, in the effort of moving up, suspended in the sound of the roaring creek as they climbed steadily higher. The rushing breezes pulsed down from the high peaks, sweeping over the snowfields, enveloping them in brief moments of shocking cold. But the sun was on them now and, with their exertions, they began to warm up. For the first time since he had left his small hut in Utah, Kelly was not focused on the hours or the days that lay in front of him. His thoughts were lost in his steps and his breathing.

They soon came to a broad snowfield that stretched two thousand feet up to the high peaks. Its slope jutted upward as it followed the steep, rocky face of the mountains to their left. The creek water fell from above in a steep tumble of sunlit-mist and spray, a transient but spectacular waterfall. To continue, they would have to cross the creek to gain the lower-angled snow field on the other side. In front of Ella, a large boulder stood several feet above the creek and, without saying a word, she stepped over to it. She placed her left boot on its highest point then scanned the creek below as well as the snow bank on the other side of the creek, which was four to five feet lower. She looked back at Kelly, then looked again at the water below, and then she jumped. With one strong push she flew easily over the creek and sank knee-deep into the soft snow on the other side. She rolled and tumbled gently in the snow for several feet. Kelly smiled. He stepped up to the rock and followed her, landing far less gracefully as he sank up to his waist in the snow and had to dig himself free. He got to his feet and walked down to her.

From here, Kelly had a better view of the steep walls of rock on the other side of the creek. The granite stretched upward as far as he could see and the sun shone brilliantly on the rock, newly wet from the melting snow. The creek rushed loudly next to them and Kelly's face tingled from the sun's early heat. He was completely immersed in the immensity and power of the landscape.

He set his rucksack next to Ella and walked about 20 feet downslope to a small shelf in the snow bank where it met the creek and formed a small pool. He knelt down and cupped his hands and took a drink of the cold water. Then he stood up and looked back at Ella, aware only of the rushing water and this girl who he'd only known for two days, but who seemed so familiar. She was gazing at the high rocks on the other side of the creek, her slight, athletic frame and long hair silhouetted against the jagged ridge of mountains. She turned her head slightly and her eyes fixed on Kelly and at the same moment a cold burst of wind flowed down the creek above them, carried all the way from the high peaks. It came onto Kelly abruptly, with the intensity and relentlessness of his past and the promise of his future. It crashed in rhythm with the falling water next to him and from it he inhaled fragments of cold granite and his tongue tasted the ocean air which had travelled thousands of miles to these mountains. Something deep in Kelly's mind, so remote it was really an ancient memory, flickered. He felt a gentle vibration pass through his body, a humming flow of energy outside his conscious intention. The heaviness of gravity was suddenly absent, leaving him with a sense of helplessness, but also a profound calm. He thought he was falling. He could only feel the cold mountain wind. His muscles tried to catch himself from something dangerous but his instincts told him he was safe.

Ella had been watching him, and bounded down in several long, plunging steps in the soft snow.

"I like drinking out of the creek, too," she said.

Kelly looked up at her. Her eyes bright and clear, reassuring and sharply focused; her long hair, vibrant in the morning sun, flowing over her right shoulder.

"Where are we?" he asked.

"It was a long time ago," Ella said. "This is where you saved me."

Kelly felt himself suspended, not even aware of his breathing. His heart momentarily paused to allow him to regain something he had lost. He felt strangely numb. He gazed back up at the high peaks and then down below to the narrow valley and its winding path out to the valley. A flame had sparked deep inside his consciousness but he could pull nothing from it, no detail, no memory of an event. But he was connected to this place. That he knew. He looked back up at Ella, searching for something that would help him understand this lost moment of his past, but it was not there. He put one knee in the snow to steady himself.

Ella was watching him intently but she said nothing. Kelly exhaled, looked again at the creek and then down to the valley, as if searching for something he had just missed.

"OK," he said to Ella softly, looking quietly at her. Then he stood up and started walking back up to his rucksack. "We should probably get going," he said.

Ella nodded. "The snow will be getting really soft soon," she said, looking up at the sky. "Oh, there's horse tails up there. Maybe there's a storm coming."

Kelly paused and looked up. He recognized the tell-tale sign of the wispy high clouds, spread like a long tail across the sky. Then he turned and looked at her quizzically. "Where did you learn all these things?" he asked.

"I don't know. I just know them."

"Maybe it's like knowing how to skip a rock across a pond," said Kelly.

Ella grinned. "Yup. I know how to do that, too."

Kelly laughed. "We make a good team," he said.

Ella nodded.

They quickly gathered their packs and began hiking upward, their boot heels swinging back and then forward into the snow. Kelly was in front and Ella followed, her feet fitting easily into the bucket-like footprints left by Kelly. They moved steadily uphill in a direct ascent of the fall line. The mountains' high point soon disappeared, the slope ahead obscuring their view. Ahead of them rose a steep, ramp-like horizon to the sky above, seemingly endless, the slope stretching skyward. It was all that they could see.

After another 200 feet of climbing, the ascent eased, and once again they could see the snow field leading to the craggy summits high above. But directly in front of them the snow was bisected by a narrow band of rock. They would have to find a way through the rocks, or over them. Kelly immediately considered them too steep and dangerous to climb directly.

"Let's see what it looks like when we get closer," Kelly said.

They walked higher and both saw an ascending sliver of snow appear to their right and disappearing into the rock band.

"Let's go look at that," Ella said, pointing to it.

"That's what I was thinking, too," Kelly replied.

They angled to the right, hiking diagonally up the snow slope. With each step, the thin ribbon of snow continued deeper into the rock band. But after walking for another minute, they could see the narrow white trail slowly reveal its unbroken path to the larger snow field above. They both saw that the snow steepened sharply near the top but it was the key they were looking for—the path to the higher terrain above and the mountain summit that they were both now committed to reach.

"What do you think?" Kelly said, glancing over at Ella as she stood looking at the path through the rocks.

"I think that's our trail," she said smiling.

"It's steep at the top," Kelly said.

"We'll be careful," Ella responded.

"Yes."

Kelly dropped his rucksack in the snow and began undoing the top flap to retrieve his water bottle. He glanced over at Ella and saw that she was already moving quickly up the slope toward the narrow chute. She looked back to see if he was following. He took a quick drink of water then put the bottle back in the rucksack. He hurriedly fastened and shouldered it, and began hiking quickly to catch up with her.

Ella was already in the chute by the time Kelly fell in step behind her. They moved quickly upward, kicking an ascending staircase in the snow, using their hands when it became steeper. By now they were about halfway up the chute, which was about 300 feet long.

Ella would pause every minute or two and glance back at Kelly. But she never said anything and Kelly was comfortable following her. He had already decided she was competent on steep snow and probably equally skilled on steep rock. They approached the upper third of the chute and the snow became harder and narrow with deep moats formed on both sides where it met the rock. Kelly and Ella both felt the snow become more tenuous. A small stream of water was running under it and they could hear its faint movement flowing over the rock, far beneath them.

Ella stopped and looked back at Kelly. "It's only another 50 feet to the top," she said.

"We should be OK," said Kelly. "Let's keep moving."

Ella immediately started climbing steadily upward again. But Kelly saw a more focused intention in her movement now. Instead of kicking once and stepping forward, she brought the heel of her foot back almost 90 degrees in a lever-like motion and swung her boot heavily into the snow, creating a deep, pocket-like step. She did that three times before committing her weight and pushing up to the next boot placement.

She was ten feet from the top when Kelly felt something shift beneath him. Then he heard a faint hollow crack release from deep in the snowpack and he instinctively tensed. The sound was almost imperceptible but it was enough to bring all of his senses alive.

"Hold up, Ella!" he called out.

The words had hardly met the mountain air when the section of snow Ella was standing on collapsed. She was tumbling backwards and Kelly could do nothing to stop it.

Ella was falling. The snow bank had fractured just above her, causing the part she had been perched on to drop through a twenty-foot hollow section and onto the rocky bed at the bottom of the chute. Kelly felt the immense crash under his feet, but his own section dropped just a few inches. He fell to his knees and planted both hands deep in the snow.

He saw Ella's boots framed against the blue sky. She was about 40 feet upslope from where he was standing. She had fallen backwards and had just cleared the lower edge of the chasm created by the collapse. Now she was speeding downhill, in the air, then on the snow. Kelly saw her try to turn herself in the air to face the slope, trying to regain some control. Then one of her boot heels hit the snow, struck hard like an arrow, and her momentum sent her cartwheeling. Kelly saw the acceleration of her fall and knew the sequence coming next was unmistakable. It flooded his consciousness—she would fall over the lower rock bands 300 feet below and then into the deep crevasses another 100 feet beyond that—probably in less than five seconds. She was going to die here, on this mountain, with him watching.

It was at once suicidal and stunningly courageous. Kelly slung his heavy rucksack from his back and in the same motion threw it toward the narrow moat, where it bounced off the edge of the snow and settled against the rock. Then he dove downhill, into Ella's path. They met instantly at a shallow angle, a soft collision of two bodies speeding downhill in a chaotic, violent tumble; their world instantly devoid of everything familiar, now only spinning fragments of snow and bright cloth and blue sky and the visceral sensation of speed and gravity. Kelly grasped for her, but they were spinning too violently, thrown against each other now and a fraction of a second later separated. She was suddenly on his left. He lunged but felt nothing. Then she was below him and he lunged again and his right palm found something. His hand locked onto it—it was one of the shoulder straps of her rucksack. He had her. Now he had to stop both of them.

He pulled Ella toward him and tried to spin to his right to point his boots downhill. Almost instantly he felt the shoulder strap pull away from her, so he extended his arm to keep them connected. Suddenly they hit a small shelf in the slope which sent them both into the air. Kelly felt the tension on the shoulder strap slacken and he guessed Ella was now above him. He reached out his feet to find purchase on the hard snow and felt his boot heel strike the slope. He locked his leg in a shallow bite, gripping the mountain and slowing them both slightly. She was directly above him now, and her eyes were bright and fearless and locked in the battle. A fraction of a second later, she was sliding past him on his left. He lurched onto his side and caught her with his arm and they both immediately spun, locked together, 100 feet above the cliff band. He rolled both of them to his right, struck one boot heel into the snow, then another. Both of them were skidding now with snow spitting into the air as their bodies bit hard into its surface and against gravity. Kelly pulled Ella on top of him and dug both elbows deep into a harder layer of snow.

The snow burned through his jacket and into his skin. Below them, the first large rock of the scattered rock band stood two feet above the snowfield surface. It looked like a small island of glistening granite. It was the first in a series of boulders that marked the entrance to a vertical drop. It was only fifty feet away now. Kelly saw it but could do nothing. His right foot glanced off the top of the rock, jarring his entire body, and they both spun to their left. But the force of the collision had slowed them slightly. Ella turned to face the slope and jammed the toes of her boots into the snow. They slowed some more. Their boots and elbows dug into the top layer of snow like grappling hooks and before either of them had time to comprehend the sudden loss of speed, they had lurched to a stop. Kelly was laying on his back and Ella was laying across the top of him, almost sideways, her head about a foot above his. She rolled to Kelly's left and dug her heels into the snow and sat up.

Her cheeks were flushed and her hair was flecked with tiny crystals of snow and ice that glinted brightly in the sun. A small streak of water dribbled down the side of her face.

They sat in silence for nearly a minute, breathing heavily, looking up the slope where they had come from.

Ella finally turned to Kelly. "Thanks for catching me," she said.

"Thanks for stopping us," Kelly answered, still not ready to move from where he sat in the snow.

The edge was only 20 feet away. They both looked below to the cliff band and saw the great void that spanned all the way to the glacier, several hundred feet below.

Kelly could hear his heart echoing through his ear drums. His breathing was rapid and shallow. He inhaled deeply and let the air release from his lungs. Then he looked up at the sky, took another deep breath, and turned to Ella.

"Are you hurt?"

"No, I'm OK. How about you?"

"I'm a little tense, but I'll get over it."

Ella laughed softly and kicked the heel of her boot into the snow.

They stayed sitting in the snow, gazing at the scene around them, orienting themselves to the world again. They looked closely at the slope above and the path they had taken. A slight trough in the snow was the only visible sign of their rapid, nearly fatal descent.

"You lost your pack," Ella said.

"I know where it is. I threw it aside up there."

"We should go find it."

"Okay, let's get moving."

They stood slowly and made their way back up to the bottom of the narrow chute, where they found the pack wedged against the rocks. They considered the terrain above, the now-missing snow bridge, and the rocky face on both sides. Without a lot of discussion, they decided they would continue upward and ascend a series of benches and cracks that were etched like calligraphy amongst the rock bands. The climbing would be exposed but not technically difficult. Kelly would go first and carry the pack. But it was getting late and first they needed to find a place to camp for the night. They would wait until the morning to climb higher. The snow would also be more firm from the cooler overnight temperatures.

"We'll be slow but deliberate," Kelly said, studying what lay ahead intently, identifying the lines of weakness in the rocky face that would take them to the top. "We will need to move with confidence but no rushing. No mistakes. Slow and steady."

"I'm a good climber," Ella said.

Kelly saw that she was apprehensive, but not afraid.

They dug and stomped out a platform in the snow with two flat rocks they found scattered on the surface of the snowfield below the rock band, evidence that falling rocks were always present up here. It was a small area they excavated in the snow, and not perfect—but it would be good enough as a place to rest, eat dinner and sleep for the night.

Chapter 10

Once the sun had fallen below the mountains to the west, the cool winds from the upper ridges and snowfields began rushing downhill across the terrain. It got cold quickly, much colder than it had been in the valley below. But Kelly and Ella huddled close together throughout the night and stayed warm that way. They built a small shelter with half of the paraglider suspended a foot above them to protect them from the wind. The rest of it lay on the ground, along with the paragliding harnesses, offering some insulation from the snow. They slept soundly for most of the night.

With the first light peeking over the mountains, they were up and moving.

Ella had made hot chocolate by melting snow and heating the water with her small stove before Kelly was awake. She set the cup on a rock beside him.

The smell of the chocolate woke him.

"Oh," he yawned. "Where did that come from?"

"I always bring hot chocolate with me," Ella answered, smiling.

Kelly took a sip. "Thank you." He handed the cup to Ella. "Please drink the rest of it."

"Chocolate is for sharing," Ella said, after taking a small sip and handing the cup back to him.

"Okay," Kelly said. "I probably won't win that argument. But I'm giving you a year's supply of it when we get out of here."

"I have a special kind that I like."

He smiled. "They should name it after you."

"You can tell them that."

"I'm going to."

"When we get out of here?"

"Yes."

They sat in idle chatter for a few minutes, finishing the hot chocolate and feeling the warmth of the sun get stronger as it rose in the sky. Then they packed up the paraglider, melted more snow for drinking water, and put away the stove and their heavier jackets as they prepared for the climb.

The route above seemed more straightforward in the morning light, the features in the rock revealing themselves more clearly.

Kelly started off and Ella watched from below. He moved slowly at first, then more steadily, until he paused on a long, horizontal section of rock that jutted out from the rock face. It allowed him to rest both feet comfortably. He gazed above him and saw at least two similar ledges along a likely route to the top. He hadn't been able to pick out these details from below but now he saw that these features would link a secure and straightforward way to the top. He could stop at each one and coach Ella until she reached him.

Ella started up. Kelly watched her closely. He quickly saw that she was confident and comfortable as a climber, finding hand and foot holds naturally, many of the same holds Kelly had used. She moved steadily up to him and joined him on the ledge.

"I shouldn't be surprised to see you do that so well. Stay focused like that and we'll get up this thing in short order."

"I like moving up like this," she answered. "It's like climbing up to heaven."

It had taken her less than five minutes to reach him. She found two large ridges of rock separated slightly from the cliff face, one at her waist and the other at eye level. She pulled on them one at a time, testing to make sure they were secure, and then she gripped them comfortably and waited for Kelly to begin climbing.

She looked over at him and saw that he was still examining the rock above.

"I think you found a good way for us to get to the top," she said. "You could probably get hired as a guide or something."

"I'm going to consider this my apprenticeship."

"I'm not sure what that means."

"It means I'm still learning."

She laughed. "Okay. Me, too."

They continued up the rock face, their movements becoming more fluid and stronger as they went, using the wide ledges to rest for a minute or two, then reaching the top and moving up again on the snow. They agreed they could reach an upper snowfield near the summit ridge in another two to three hours by climbing up a couloir. The couloir was a few hundred feet wide at the bottom apron but narrowed to about 80 feet near the top. The angle was gentle at the entrance but it steepened to nearly 60 degrees at the top.

They were halfway up the couloir when Ella noticed the wide wisps of moisture lying in thin, white brush strokes against the vibrant blue of the sky. They stretched like white streamers far above even the highest peaks.

She pointed to the sky. "Mr. Guide, a storm is coming," she said.

Kelly stopped and looked up to see the unmistakable sign of high-altitude moisture and strong winds; the leading edge of a much bigger weather front approaching from the west. He knew immediately that their world was going to change in the next 24 hours, it was only a matter of how much wind and moisture they would experience and how cold it would get. Kelly's mind ran through the options they had for fashioning a shelter. They had the paraglider. The fabric could be used to create a strong tent if it was staked deep in the snow with rocks. But it would likely still leave them very exposed to cold and wind, and if it snowed it would accumulate quickly on top of them. The other option was some kind of snow cave. They had nothing to dig with but they might be able to find some rocks to shovel and excavate the snow. They could also retreat—start to head back down the way they came. But it was late and Kelly knew they would need the time they had before the storm's arrival to begin building a shelter or risk getting caught out in high wind and the cold. Even though he thought it was unlikely, he knew snow was a possibility. If enough of it accumulated quickly, the potential for an avalanche was high given the existing snowpack. Any new snow on top of it would be highly unstable. Kelly didn't know how long the storm would take to arrive in their mountains, maybe they had enough time to descend all the way to the canyon below—but he didn't ponder on the risk they would be taking. He ruled it out immediately.

They reached the top of the couloir in another 30 minutes. As they came over the steep lip where it met the snowfield, they saw for the first time the complex topography of the upper mountain. They had been on a steady climb on the lower slopes for two days, able to see only the steep terrain in front of them. What greeted them now was a different world. The snowfield spread out in front of them on a broad shoulder for several hundred feet in both directions, scattered with small islands of rock, rising three to ten feet above the snow. Above this broad field, the slope rose up sharply to a series of very steep chutes and narrow, rocky spines that all ascended to the summit. A cathedral of rock, snow and ice, all touching the sky. The summit itself was a thin promontory, resembling a spire—a remote and unreachable island that seemed more a part of the sky than the earth.

Ella and Kelly both walked across this new landscape. They were only a few feet apart, but wandering forward separately and slowly, each drawn forward by the sight before them. Kelly walked to his right where the snowfield abutted the rocks. He was scanning them for a spot that might be suitable for a snow cave. He sensed that Ella was no longer near him. He looked over his shoulder and saw her standing frozen in the middle of the snowfield, about fifty feet away.

"There's a cabin up here," Ella shouted, as if she were speaking to the sky rather than to Kelly.

She turned to her right, walked a few feet and stopped. Kelly watched her, wondering if he had misunderstood what she had said.

She cast her eyes to the scattered rocky outcroppings in front of her. Then she turned and faced the other direction. She shifted her weight to the heel of her right foot. She tilted her head back and gazed at the sky and Kelly saw that her eyes were closed. Then she opened them and looked at the snowy landscape and the scattered jagged rocks, patches of snow still draping some of them. She immediately began walking uphill toward a high, long section of rock that jutted out from a series of low rocky berms. She walked slowly at first, her head swiveling side to side as her eyes scanned the world around her, as though she was checking on the correctness of some work she had just completed. Then she accelerated. Without breaking stride, she turned and looked behind her and saw Kelly rooted in the snow.

"It's this way, come on!" she shouted.

There was something in the conviction of Ella's movement that kept Kelly silently watching. He remained still and waited a few seconds to see if she would pause, maybe to check her surroundings again, to confirm her instincts once more, or to orient herself by the terrain around her. But she kept walking, sometimes even breaking into a run. Kelly cocked his head sideways, momentarily unsure of what was happening. Then he began following her.

Ella reached the downhill edge of the rocks that stretched outward like a long finger on the surface of the snow. She continued past them. Kelly was twenty feet behind her and he could now see a large, bowl-shaped area revealing itself on the other side of the rocks, extending back in toward the base of the mountain. It was about the size of a football field and protected on all sides by rock benches and wind-blown berms of snow. Some of them were as high as 50 feet. The area seemed remarkably out of place—a well-protected harbor in an otherwise steep and exposed landscape.

There was obviously no cabin, though. It was a place of rock and snow far above tree line in a hostile alpine environment. Kelly didn't doubt that Ella felt a strong connection to this place but he also knew memories can play out as disconnected fragments of a person's past. He thought that Ella had probably been here before and this was part of a need to reconnect an event in her life—but he also knew the cabin she was looking for existed somewhere else, maybe in a place she had known when she was very young. But right now it was time for them to begin the work of building a shelter if they were going to be protected from the storm that was coming. The sky told the story. The wispy clouds had given way to upper-level cumulus, stretched by the strong winds and appearing like gigantic lenses in the atmosphere. The dangerous high winds would soon reach them. Kelly looked upward and felt a surge of anxiety. He stopped following Ella's boot tracks.

"Ella, we need to find a place to dig a snow cave."

But she kept on walking toward the interior of the mountain.

"I know she heard me," Kelly said to himself softly. For an instant he thought to yell again more loudly. But he knew it wouldn't change anything. She was going to keep walking. He didn't know a lot about this girl, but he knew that.

And she did keep walking, directly toward the boundary of rock and snow that separated this refuge from the steep and more dangerous reaches of the upper mountain.

Kelly knew that Ella had her own way of doing things, and even if he might be initially puzzled by what she did, she had always demonstrated that she was capable, and probably gifted with insight. Kelly had no answer for what Ella was doing now, at least in the time he had to consider it.

So, he began following her, because in this moment nothing else made sense.

As he trudged through the snow, Kelly sensed Ella was reconnecting with her past and when

he looked up he saw that she was moving even faster. Kelly felt a constriction in the pit of his stomach. His body was telling him that they should be building a shelter. But then, within the rocky bench a hundred feet in front of Ella, a peculiar line revealed itself amongst the rocks, a fragment of a shape which Kelly's eyes instinctively picked up.

Ella continued walking towards it, her red jacket gaining height against the rocky bench in front of her.

An unnatural line in the distant rocks rose vertically and as he walked closer, Kelly could trace it higher and now saw it was connected with another straight line and that one split off to the left at 90 degrees. Below the line were uniform grey stones, each about the size of a small cutting board. They were stacked off-center and ran down to a cement footing at the base of the rock bench. Kelly's cognition caught up with the image before him and he realized he was looking at a carefully constructed stone hut. It was about ten-feet high and twenty-feet wide.

Ella was now running. As she approached the hut she veered left, bounded up on the rocky bench in two easy strides, and disappeared around the corner. Kelly followed her and found her standing in front of a slate-grey metal door with a large metal latch. She lifted it up, shoved the door open, and grinned back at Kelly.

"I told you," Ella said, as she disappeared inside the hut.

Kelly approached the door then paused. He looked closely at the walls of the hut. Each stone had been cleanly cut and mortar filled the cracks between them. The cement footing on the bench looked perfectly level. The bench itself rose about twenty feet above the snowfield, free of the sloughing avalanches that were sure to release from the high ridges behind it. He looked up the steep narrow spines of the aretes that led to the summit 800 feet above. They were almost vertical. Snow-filled chutes bordered the aretes, all meeting at a final narrow ridge that led to the summit, which was now no more than 100 feet across and 20 feet wide. Toward the west where they had ascended, the snowfield dropped away several thousand feet. A broad valley could be seen even farther in the distance, with open fields dotted with the occasional farmhouses, about 15 miles away. Kelly gazed back at their route to this point and thought it would be difficult to descend in bad weather, especially with fresh snow or limited visibility. He looked farther west to the large valley and saw that the sky had become a blue-black slate of dark clouds, marching above the valley, distant still but deceptive in their speed.

As Kelly turned to enter the hut he felt the first bite of the cold air. He knew the storm could be on them within an hour.

Ella was already kneeling at the door of a small wood stove, stacking kindling and stuffing old newspaper under the teepee-shaped pile of wood she had built inside the stove. The stove sat along the far wall of the mostly empty hut. Two sleeping cots were arranged along the two end walls, with a pile of wool blankets stacked on top of each. A canvas bag and a small wooden box filled with kindling sat along the near wall next to the door. The ceiling was supported by a large timber that ran lengthwise through the center. Rough timber framing ran down from the beam to the side walls, which were built with stone and mortar. Tightly fitted flagstone, cut from the mountain, was laid on the floor where tiny rivers of sand meandered between their edges. Kelly had noticed the roof as he approached the hut—it was slate-grey metal and camouflaged almost perfectly by the granite landscape that surrounded it. The hut was essentially invisible where it sat against the mountain rocks, but for the lines of its roof.

"I knew it was here. I just couldn't remember exactly where... until I got here," Ella said. She was still sitting by the small stove. Its door was open, revealing an orange blaze of light and heat, the dry pine sticks crackling in the flames.

She skooched back and sat against the far wall as Kelly stepped inside the hut.

"I believed you were going somewhere important but I couldn't imagine this," he said. He dropped his rucksack by the door. "Where did you find the firewood?"

"It's on the outside wall covered in tarps. There's stacks of it. And it looks like there's a few other things in this canvas bag. There are two snow shovels outside along the back wall."

Kelly went outside and took an armful of dry pine in his arms. Then he came back inside and lay them near the stove. He handed one piece to Ella, who placed it carefully on the burning pile.

Kelly moved over to one of the cots and sat on its edge.

Ella kicked off her boots and took a drink from her water bottle.

"I think we'll be warmer tonight," Kelly said smiling.

"This old stove won't let us down," Ella replied, and laughed.

"How did you know this was here?"

"I used to stay here with my parents a long time ago. They would carry me up in their kid-carry pack and we'd spend the night watching the stars. My parents would tell me stories about the mountain ghosts that live up here, who help climbers during bad storms. We'd stay outside until it got too cold and then we'd come in and build a fire. We would usually stay for a couple days, so that we could gather firewood from the forest below and bring it up."

As Kelly listened, he gazed up at the large wooden beam that spanned the length of the hut.

"I think the mountain ghosts must have built this hut," Ella said.

Kelly laughed and walked to the door to examine the walls. He ran his hand along the smooth stone where it had been cut to fit the dimensions of the framed door. He looked at the tight joints of the frame and swung the door shut. It glided with its own weight cleanly into the frame where there was no discernible gap. He began to consider the tools and the time and skill it must have taken to construct something so detailed and with such challenging and heavy material. The more he considered it, the more the idea of the hut became something extraordinary, almost mythical.

He pushed the door open, hopped down off the rocks and into the soft snow. His boots sank into the first five inches with a gentle sensation of skiing that made Kelly smile. He walked forward another 100 feet and looked out to the valley. The sky, the far side of the valley, had the first hint of snowfall hidden in a veil of bluish-black clouds, pushing out the last of the light. From the west, a cold gust of wind swept up the mountain. Kelly turned away just as it caught the hood of his jacket and lashed his cheek. He tucked his head down against the wind and began walking back to the hut, which even from this distance seemed to symbolize this mountain range—elegant and unruly at the same time. He wondered if Ella had been right about the ghosts.

Kelly walked back and climbed back up over the boulders, their flat surface offering wide, majestic steps leading to the hut. He walked around to the back wall where he gathered another small bundle of firewood in his arms. When he walked through the open door of the hut, he was warmed by the comfort of a resolute shelter and its protection from the elements.

But there was no Ella. He had wanted to warn her about the approaching snow, but the hut was empty. She must have gone out to collect snow to melt for drinking water, he thought, but he hadn't seen her on his way back to the hut. And regardless of how ordinary and explainable her absence might be, there was a familiar tug of anxiousness deep in his chest. He bent down on one knee and placed the wood on the floor next to the stove, then closed the small stove door when a sharp gust of wind swept the outside walls of the hut, making the door swing shut quickly with a heavy thud. The slam of the door unsettled Kelly. He knew it was just the wind, pulling on the door the way a river eddy pulls a drifting swimmer, but that didn't ease his disquiet. He stood up, walked over to his cot, and grabbed his heavy jacket. Then he turned back toward the door, throwing one arm through a sleeve and then the other, quickly wrapping the jacket around his body. He felt the cold pushing its way into the hut as he reached for the door latch, his mind now focused on locating Ella.

But a flash of color in front of him pulled something from his past, disorienting him. He stopped and fixed his gaze on it for several seconds before his mind registered what it was.

It was hanging from a small, rusted metal ring at eye level in the middle of the door and was tied in a figure of eight. Kelly reached out and ran his fingers along the edges of the red ribbon. Then he pushed it out of his mind. He had to find Ella.

He swung the door open and the wind pushed him back in a pulsing wave. A few dry snowflakes lashed his eyes. He winced and instinctively lowered his head before stepping carefully across the rocks. He turned left, more out of instinct than anything else. As he moved, he scanned the rocky bench in front of him and the slopes below. The scale of the landscape in front of him was immense; a sea of rocky ridges and vast snow fields stretching downward to the river. But there was no sign of Ella. He kept walking for several hundred feet, following the high point of the bench which led to the south. Snow was now starting to accumulate on the rocks and Kelly chose his steps carefully, placing his feet on the flat parts of the stones and boulders. He climbed up to the highest point along the bench, which rose above the snow slopes like the prow of a ship pushing into the ocean.

From here he had a commanding view of everything in front of him—but still there was no sign of Ella. She was not on the bench or below it, and Kelly now had to think that something had gone wrong. He felt sick in the pit of his stomach. She could have slipped on the rocks and skidded down a steep section of the snow. She could have tumbled for thousands of feet, he knew. He would need to descend and start searching and that probably meant spending the night without shelter, exposed to the storm. It was already snowing heavily. Curtains of white, dancing streamers moved over the slopes, some touching the ground and others pushing up the mountain and disappearing among the dark shapes of the ridgelines. He feared the worst as he headed back to the hut to retrieve his rucksack. But he had only travelled about twenty feet before he stopped suddenly and turned toward the upper mountain. Balancing carefully on a steep portion of a large boulder, at first his eyes moved over the steep rocky spine too quickly, his mind unconsciously dismissing it as too steep. But when he looked again the human shape stood out, and it was unmistakable.

Chapter 11

It took Kelly 10 minutes of careful climbing before he was at the same height as Ella. The rock wasn't vertical, but it was steep enough that a slip and fall would be fatal. When he was 100 feet across from her, he saw that she was perched on a small ledge. Her face was turned to the wind and snow as the fabric of her nylon pants and jacket flapped loudly, woven into the sounds of the wind. Blowing eddies of snow coming up the rock face were building small dunes at her feet. They streamed over her boots and covered her ankles. She looked completely at peace.

Kelly knew that she must be very cold, but she showed no sign of this, or of any intent to leave the ledge. She didn't seem to notice him, or at least he could not tell if she had. Her jacket flashed in strokes of muted red as the wind and snow swept over her. She was as much amongst the rock and snow as any living thing could be. It occurred to Kelly that that he should be nervous, seeing her so exposed, but for some reason he wasn't. He placed his gloved hand on the rock face to his left, adjusted his left boot for balance, and took a deep breath.

Ella remained rooted to the rock. Kelly saw her gaze sweeping across the rocks and snowfield below. Then she tilted her head slightly, as if she was listening for something. The gusts were slowly losing strength, and the calm lulls between them became longer. Within a few minutes, the rushing of the wind was mostly gone and the quiet that followed felt strangely transient, like a void waiting to be filled by the sky.

Ella swung her rucksack off one shoulder and latched onto it with both hands. She unclipped the top lid and pulled a red, wooden box from the rucksack. She held it at her waist and let it sit there in her extended palms for nearly a minute, her head bowed in a steady gaze. Then she brought her eyes back to the snowfields and the landscape below. She removed the lid of the box and, without hesitating, swung her right arm straight back behind her and extended it up above her shoulder. She swung the box down and forward in a quick, long sweeping arc that sent its contents outward.

The ashes met the air as a light grey stream against the opaque sky, suspended high above the snowfield for just two seconds as Ella watched them rise, slowly at first, and then rapidly up toward the high peak behind her, carried by the wind pushing up against the rock face. Ella turned and watched them expand and then disappear, losing sight of their color and shape a hundred feet above her. She continued to watch them for another minute. Then she turned and looked directly at Kelly, and smiled.

She knew I was here all along, he said to himself.

Ella put the box back in her rucksack and swung it onto her back. Then she turned and looked at the rocks and the steep face that led back the way she had come. Any surface that was remotely flat was covered in snow. She began moving down, slowly at first, but without hesitation. She knew going down was always more dangerous than climbing up.

A steeply angled rock face met her as she approached Kelly. It stretched twenty feet to the small outcrop where he stood. It was nearly vertical, the rock appearing to possess few useable foot and handholds. A small ledge, about a foot wide, sat 10 feet above at the top of the face, covered in snow. Ella scanned the rock and the area above and below it. She quickly dismissed the alternative routes above and below as being too uncertain and even more dangerous than the one in front of her.

Her eyes met Kelly's briefly and she took a deep breath then looked quickly at her boots. She kicked them hard against the rocks and started across the face, using the grip of her boots to keep her from sliding. The bare palms of her hands, pressed down on the granite, kept her balanced. A slip would likely mean a fall and a fall would be fatal. Both she and Kelly knew that. He watched intently, staying silent.

Ella moved gracefully and without discernable tension in her body, her feet and hands intuitively finding ridges and holds in the rock. She was comfortable and poised, every movement precise and measured. Flurries of snow shrouded her briefly, but it was dry and not slippery when it landed on the rock. She blew it off the rock in easy exhales and it came free like fine powder. Five feet below her, a small outcrop of rock protruded out, angled at 45 degrees. It was perhaps three feet across. Besides that, only empty space lay below her.

The sharp granite stung her skin and the cold pulled the warmth from her fingers and palms, numbing them. But her movements were clean in spite of the pain and she kept her weight carefully distributed between her two feet and her hands. She never put too much of her body in any one place while still moving and leveraging her weight laterally across the face, in a delicate dance with gravity

Then a boot slipped.

A tiny ridge where Ella's left toe was perched broke. At the same time her left arm was moving diagonally across the face, her palm free of the rock, making her suddenly vulnerable to gravity. Ella was sliding off the face. Her mind and body, if they reacted perfectly and without hesitation, would give her a chance. But only instinct could save her. And courage. It was ten feet across to the ledge where

Kelly was standing and she would need to jump it. Ella had vaulted farther than that in gymnastics practice once. And once, with her friend Amy, she had jumped over a creek as wide.

But this wasn't a creek where a slip would mean falling into the water and walking home in soaking wet clothes. It was a steep mountain face, high above a remote snowfield, far from civilization and any help. Separating herself from the rock that she still had a hand and one boot gripped on, even if tenuous, would be a radical idea.

The mind is slow to accept a massive risk. The hope of a safer path, even it's very small, is hard to extinguish in most people. They take the risk as a last resort, if they do it all. Most will instinctively resort to risk avoidance in the face of huge uncertainty. They hesitate. Unless they're bold.

And Ella was bold.

Years later, if someone had asked Kelly to describe what he saw in that instant, he would describe the subtle red of Ella's jacket in the blowing snow, the flinty smell of the air's static electricity on the rock, the pulsing brace of the wind on his face and the sharp granite that his left hand was gripping. He would remember the penetrating cold reaching through his jacket, and the indelible image of Ella framed against the sky and what she did next.

She turned toward Kelly, her left shoulder now perpendicular to the drop below her. Then her right knee dropped under her so that the outside of her right thigh came flat against the sloping face of the rock. She reached her right arm upward, stretching above her head, her palm flat against the rock. The empty space to her left was only slightly visible in the corner of her eye but she felt it there, a dangerous presence beside her, waiting for her to stumble. The toe of her right boot, the only thing still gripping the rock, was sliding down the face. She had abandoned her attachment to the rock, as tenuous as it was. She was completely committed.

Kelly turned directly toward Ella. He moved his right foot to the outside of the ledge. In the pit of his stomach a hollow, hard ache took hold.

It was her right knee lifting up along the face of the wall that Kelly saw most distinctly. It rose above her right hip, where her right foot found a high spot on the rock. Her boot gripped a small piece of the face and it put her slightly off balance. It wasn't much leverage for what she did next, but it was enough. Kelly saw her for a brief second, suspended, held by the propulsion of her body. And then in one spectacular instant she launched into the air and flew down to the ledge where he stood.

It didn't occur to him that he would not be able to stop her or hold on to her, that he might be knocked off balance and the pending crash would send them both tumbling off the rock face into the empty space below them. It would have occurred to others, had they heard the story repeated later, in a restaurant or bar—but for both Ella and Kelly that thought was vacant from their minds.

Kelly knew instinctively that he could only stop Ella with the strength of his stance, that trying to grip the rock face with one arm and catch her with the other would be impossible. He would need to catch her with both arms, while somehow staying on the ledge.

Ella was only aware of being weightless and the raw energy of the cold air filling her lungs and the sharp, wind-driven snow giving her a gentle lift. There was no fear or sense of dread. Her world had narrowed and both her mind and body sensed only what they needed to do to survive. Nothing else mattered but this single movement, a spontaneous flight to escape death. She had to do it right. She knew she needed to be perfect in where her feet landed, what her eyes captured, how her legs absorbed the energy of her landing and what she grabbed the instant her feet hit the ledge. But she also knew none of that would matter if Kelly could not hold onto her. For good reason, she didn't question that.

Her right foot landed first. She was still accelerating as Kelly leaned forward to absorb her energy and tilted back to catch her just under her left arm, which was raised high as if reaching for the sky. The impact shook him but he felt the life of her body in his grasp now. His stance shifted with the force but he quickly placed his feet in a stronger position on the ledge than before. He let her momentum swing both of them out to the face. Kelly's right foot rooted to the ledge and swung them like a barn door, his right arm hooked under Ella's left armpit. He reached around her and found a strap from her pack. His fingers tightened hard around it instantly.

He pulled it toward him while still swinging them both to the right, letting her momentum bring them both around to the far side of the rock face like a wheel turning on its axle.

They slammed into the face with Ella against the rock and Kelly pinned against her. He shuffled his feet to secure them both but didn't release his grip. Ella was crouched low, her knees bent, her weight centered down on the ledge. She looked out to the snowfields below and the blowing snow rising and falling around them. She felt the solid face against her back and let her feet sink down in her boots to the ground.

"Are you OK?" Kelly asked.

Ella looked up at him and nodded. "Better than I was a second ago."

Kelly laughed softly and said, "We should probably get down to the cabin, someplace warm—and flat."

"With hot chocolate."

"Yes."

Kelly turned to look down at the cabin. It looked peaceful with the blowing snow sweeping over the roof and spilling dry, light piles along the walls. He saw the smoke from the woodstove rising from the chimney and how the wind made it rise above the roof and then disappear like vapor. And in one heavy exhale, his muscles relaxed and he placed his right hand on the rock wall just above Ella's head. They both stood up slowly, gaining their balance on the ledge.

They traversed in a gradual descent to the snowfield. The wind was now leaving small drifts that rose over their boots.

As they reached the cabin, Ella had to kick away a pile of snow to open the cabin door. Kelly gathered another armful of wood while she went inside. She sat on one of the cots, took off her boots, and put her socks on the stone floor next to the stove to let them dry. Thin ribbons of steam began to rise from them.

Then she gathered all the remaining food from their rucksacks and laid it out on the floor near the back wall as Kelly came inside and set the firewood down next to the stove.

Kelly looked at the three small cans of tuna and two remaining energy bars laid out on the floor.

"It could be worse," he said. "At least some small creature didn't come in here and steal what we had left."

"Little creatures have to eat, too," Ella said.

"Are you sure you didn't get hurt up there?" Kelly asked her.

"I'm good as new," Ella said. "My elbow hit the rock kind of hard but it's only bruised. My parents will always be here now. I like that."

"Those were your parents' ashes that you scattered?"

"Yes, some of them. The rest I spread along their favorite rapid in Thunder Creek."

Ella moved down off the cot and sat on the stone floor near the stove. She listened to the cracking of the dry wood burning and put her hands out to feel its heat. After a minute, she stood and walked over to the door in her bare feet before opening it and stepping outside. A gust of wind filled the cabin with dry, powdery snow. Some landed on the far side of the cabin floor and quickly evaporated in the heat. Ella stood just outside the door, looking up to the sky and the blowing snow.

After a few seconds she came back inside the cabin and latched the door with a solid *thunk* and then sat on the floor near the stove. She knocked the dry snow from her feet and then stretched her legs out and let the heat of the stove warm her bare feet.

"Did you see how the wind carried their ashes all the way to the top of the mountain?'

"I lost sight of them," Kelly said. "I think they just kept following the mountain all the way up, and then they went beyond it."

"I think so, too," Ella said smiling.

A strong gust of wind rushed over the roof and they both looked up. Even in the fading light they could see the blowing snow dancing outside the small window on the west side of the cabin.

Kelly found two small candles in the canvas bag behind one of the cots and he lit them with a piece of burning kindling he drew from the stove. He set one candle near the door and the other on the floor in the middle of the room and then sat on the edge of his cot.

The flame flickered brightly against the stone floor.

Ella stretched her legs out toward the stove and pulled her pack down from the cot. She leaned back against it, pulling her pant legs up above her knees and feeling the heat of the stove on her skin.

"I can go back down now," she said.

Kelly looked over at her. "Were your parents as brave as you?" he said.

Ella laughed warmly. "Yes, I learned to be brave from them," she said. "But my dad said I was too brave sometimes. I miss them. But somehow, it's not as bad now. It seems easier."

"It's easier because you made it that way," Kelly said.

"You think that's true?"

"Yes."

"We can start down tomorrow morning if the snow is not too deep," Kelly said. "If it keeps snowing it will be dangerous. We can see in the morning."

He opened a can of tuna, pulled his water bottle from his pack, and handed both to Ella. Then he unwrapped one of the energy bars, broke off a small piece, and put it in his mouth.

Ella slowly ate small pieces of tuna with a fork she pulled from her pack.

"Thanks for catching me up there," she said.

"I was happy to do it," Kelly said laughing. "But no more flying for a while, please."

"I was scared, but I knew I could do it."

"I know. It was brilliant."

They finished eating and Kelly went to the door and stepped outside, keeping the door slightly ajar. He stepped back into the doorway, kicked the snow off his boots, and came back inside and closed the door.

"The wind has died down a bit but it's still snowing out there. I can't see any stars."

"It didn't look like it wanted to stop," Ella said. Then she turned to him. "How do you feel? We're both so hungry now. It seems worse at night when I'm not moving."

"It's the same for me," Kelly said. "Eat the rest of this." He reached over to Ella with the last piece of the energy bar.

"Let's save it for tomorrow," she said, and she tucked it into her rucksack. "Let's not talk about food anymore tonight."

"We can talk about something else," Kelly said.

Ella pushed her rucksack behind her and let it lay flat on the stone floor and then lay her head and shoulders on it and stretched her legs out. "Where will you go after we leave the mountains? Igbn a year from tonight, where will you be living?" she asked.

"I think I know," Kelly said, sitting on the edge of his cot close to the heat of the stove. "I've never been there. But I can show you on a map."

Kelly reached into his rucksack and found the card that Ana had sent him.

He handed it to Ella.

"This is really pretty, how carefully this is drawn," Ella said. "Where is this?"

"It's a mountain range in Europe. I have a friend who is going to be living there. I think she must have lived there before, in the house with the letter A next to it."

"She drew this map for you?"

"Yes," Kelly said.

"But you don't know if you will be there?"

"If I find her there then I will be there."

"She will be there," Ella said.

Ella sat up and pulled her rucksack over to her and unzipped the top compartment and began searching through it. She found a plastic bag and opened it and pulled out several colored pencils and a large sheet of paper.

She laid the paper on a large stone in front of her and placed the card above the paper. Then she picked up a dark blue pencil and began drawing, starting from the middle of the paper and working out, replicating the map that Ana had drawn.

Kelly watched as Ella included every detail of the card. When she was done, she handed the paper to Kelly.

"This is much better than anything I could have done," he said. "I can only add one thing." He reached out his hand to Ella and she handed him the pencil. Kelly took it and wrote a series of numbers in the margin of the paper and another set directly below it.

"That's my telephone number and Ana's number is the second one," Kelly said as he handed the paper and pencil back to Ella. "You can find both of us with that."

"Her name is Ana?"

"Yes."

Kelly picked up his jacket from the cot and unzipped the chest pocket. He pulled out a photo he had taken in Thailand and handed it to Ella. Ana was sitting on Kelly's porch, wearing a black tank top and a pair of thin, loose-fitting light-blue cotton pants with the cuffs rolled up to her knees, her feet propped up on a small table. She was reading a book, seemingly unaware that her photo was being taken.

"She's beautiful," Ella said. "Would she want me to visit?"

"She would be disappointed if you didn't."

"Does Ana ski?"

"Yes. I think she is a good skier."

"If I came to visit, do you think she would take me skiing?"

"She would love to take you skiing."

"Well, I guess it's settled then, we both know where we will be next year," Ella said smiling.

"I know you're good with navigating but let us take care of the travel arrangements," Kelly said.

"That sounds nice," Ella said.

Ella stood up and put another piece of wood in the stove and Kelly retrieved the wool blankets that they had found in the hut when they first arrived. They pushed their two cots together and pulled the blankets over them and went to sleep.

Chapter 12

They both heard the storm crashing throughout the night. Sometimes it was so distant and so faint it was hard to know if it was the wind pushing against the cliffs or something created by their deep tiredness, an apparition residing between dreams and consciousness. At other times the sound was so close it was like thunder and the cabin shook. It felt like the thick wooden timbers would be crushed and the cabin carried down the mountain.

Ella woke early with the sound of another cascading roar from high above them. She went to the door, unlatched the metal bar, and pulled the door in slowly. But when she saw the rising wall of snow standing behind it, she slowly closed it again to keep from disturbing it.

Kelly stirred with the sound of the door.

"The snow never did stop," Ella said.

Kelly swung his legs out from the cot, stepped into his boots without lacing them, and walked to the door. They looked at each other quickly as Ella opened it again slowly. A knee-high drift rose straight up from the bottom of the door frame. Ella pushed outward into the snow with the instep of her boots and her lower legs, kicking from the top down to keep the drift out of the cabin.

Then she stepped outside and sunk up to her thighs. Light was revealing the mountains now and the large drifts of snow that had formed overnight. Ella looked back at Kelly.

"Well, it could be worse," she said. "The cabin could be buried."

"I'm going to go take a look around," Kelly said.

He went back to his cot, threw his jacket on, and laced his boots. Then he stepped through the doorway and into the space that Ella had kicked clear. He paused to listen. The mountains were remarkably quiet now. He moved out farther and stood on the lip of the rock bench just ten feet from the cabin door. He looked first at the sky and even though it was still early morning, he saw signs of the night's storm passing out of the valley. Directly overhead, the clouds were thinner than yesterday.

He zipped his jacket and pulled up its hood, then stepped off the bench. The snow was hollow there and he sunk to his waist in a small moat that had formed between the bench and the snowfield. Struggling and swinging his torso and arms back and forth, he managed to move out of the sunken space and reach the snowfield just a few feet below the bench.

Kelly's progress was more like swimming than walking. But he continued for another 100 feet before stopping at a place where he could view the mountains and the valley. Now he was sure the storm had passed to the east. He turned to look at the jagged peak above and had a good view of the couloirs and ridges. Anything that was not vertical was blanketed in heavy snow. A few scattered tendrils of moisture were lifting out of the steep chutes before disappearing against the rocky face. In two of the large gullies the snow was scraped clean, sent downhill in large avalanches. The valley below was still obscured with low clouds. Kelly examined it all closely, knowing that he and Ella had few options. The air was cold even without the penetrating wind, but the walk had warmed him and he stood quietly for several minutes, listening for avalanches or any hint of wind. But everything remained still. It was a changed landscape now. Very different from just a day ago. It was a world that would permit travel only with a massive amount of risk and hardship. He looked closely at the snowfield directly in front of him, gauging its angle and length before it fell away to the steep slopes below. He estimated the slope ran about 200 feet before becoming nearly vertical. The upper part looked like a moderately steep driveway. He turned and began walking back to the cabin and even though moving was easier now on the path he had created, he realized for the first time since the plane crash that he was very weak.

Ella watched him from the edge of the rock bench. She was leaning against the wooden handle of one of the snow shovels, which was sunk deep sunk into the lip of the rock bench, like a fence post. Kelly saw that a patio size area around the cabin had been shoveled free of snow.

Kelly had immediately realized when he left the cabin that moving in the deep snow would be time-consuming. Returning to the cabin was easier but it still took him several minutes to cover the last thirty feet to where Ella was standing.

He walked to the edge of the rock bench and Ella reached out her hand and helped him up the last step.

They both stood there on the bench for a moment, Kelly resting and Ella watching as the sun continued to burn away the thin cloud. Faint rays of light were now bringing some warmth to their skin.

"You should eat the rest of the energy bar," Kelly said. "You shouldn't wait too long or you will get too weak."

Ella pulled her jacket tight around her and tucked her hands into her sleeves.

"No," she said, looking directly at Kelly. "We only have one bar and two cans of tuna left. I can wait. We need to save it for hiking out. I know we're stuck here... for a while."

A muffled, distant crash rose from the highest point of the mountain. They both turned and looked.

The sound got louder until it was like artillery exploding. Then large, broken plates of snow and white dust shattered against the rocks on a far ridgeline, moving rapidly down a steep face. It was an avalanche. It was too far away to reach the cabin but the appearance of this new threat, a challenge to anyone who dared travel on these slopes, sent a chill through them. It was also delivering a simple message: their only course of action was no action at all. They were, in every sense of the word, trapped.

Kelly turned and walked back into the cabin. He found the rucksack where the food was packed. He retrieved one of the energy bars and then gathered up the fabric of the paraglider and folded it and placed it back in its bag before coming back outside.

He handed the energy bar to Ella. She shook her head.

"We're not staying here," he said.

"You've always been sensible... as long as I've known you..." Ella said. "I think you need to eat this." She pointed to the food in his hand. "Then you can start making sense again."

Kelly laughed. "So how long *have* we known each other?"

"I was five years old," she said.

Kelly looked at her, at the soft but brilliant energy in her eyes. His gaze shifted down and then past Ella to the valley. Then he turned quickly and walked out on the flat bench toward the valley.

"We were up here," he said, stopping.

"My parents were lost in the avalanche and you found me."

He turned back to her. "I didn't know if..." Kelly said quietly, and his voice trailed off. He walked to the edge of the bench and sat in the snow with his legs resting off the lip of the bench.

Ella came over and sat next to him.

"You found me walking on the snowfield and we walked down the mountain together. You were wearing one of those black visor hats and blue pants. You asked about my parents but I couldn't tell you anything."

Kelly sat and listened, his eyes on Ella and then looking out to the valley.

"You had a small water bottle and you kept asking me to drink," she went on. "I remember my skin hurt from the sun and you had some lotion that you put on my face and hands. We had to cross the creek but there were still snow banks and we weren't in the forest yet. The water was too deep so you picked me up and carried me across it."

Ella paused and looked down to the thin ribbon of water that was visible as it carved through the snowfield 1000 feet below them.

"What happened? I just remember bits and pieces," Kelly said. "I remember there was an avalanche and I remember you on the snow bank, and your red jacket. It has never left me. But I could not remember what had happened and sometimes I thought it was just parts of my dreams that were coming back to me."

"Your boot slipped on the rocks and the water caught you. I remember feeling things drop really fast. We lunged toward the bank and then I was thrown forward to the snow. When I looked back I saw you falling into the water, and then you were gone."

"I couldn't get to the other side," Kelly said. He paused and looked at Ella. His mind had been assembling the images, the fragments of memory, and those pieces that he thought he had lost. "I've had this dream so many times, that I lost you but I couldn't place what was real..."

"I ran down the bank and looked for you," Ella said. "And then it got dark and I slept by the creek and the next day I kept walking down and I saw a trail so I walked on that and I thought you might be there. But some hikers found me."

"I came out of the creek in the forest but I couldn't remember anything," Kelly said.

"But you made it out of the mountains. And then... up here, I found you after all," she said smiling.

"I always believed you were alive," Kelly said.

"I was. And so were you," Ella said.

Kelly looked at Ella and smiled again. He tilted his head back and gazed up to the sky and the thinning clouds and he saw faint streaks of chalky blue sky.

"You still have a red jacket," he said.

Ella laughed and said, "Yes, a couple sizes bigger now. I bought this one last year," she said as she tugged on the collar of her jacket.

Ella kicked the heels of her boots against the snow bank and the lip sloughed off and rolled onto the slope below. They both watched it slide downhill. As it moved, it gathered more snow and quickly became a small avalanche. They watched it disappear below a rise, 200 feet below. The sound of snow collapsing and rushing downhill faded.

"How can we get out of here?" Ella said, almost to herself.

"We will."

"I'm sorry I got you stuck up here."

Kelly watched her look down the mountain with her head slightly bowed.

"You didn't get us stuck up here. The mountains did that when they let the snow fall."

Ella looked up and laughed softly. "I'm getting so hungry."

"I know. Me, too."

She leaned back, braced herself back in the snow, and looked over at Kelly.

"I have an idea," he said.

"Eat all of our food?"

Kelly laughed and propped himself in the snow like Ella. "Something better than that. Come on, let's go back to the cabin."

They pushed themselves up and began walking back. It wasn't far and the snow here had been cleared. But Kelly still stumbled. His legs buckled when one of his boots sunk sideways. He didn't have the strength to counter the sudden shift, as minor as it was. Ella saw him and stopped.

"I'm OK. I just need to walk slower," he said. "I'm a little light-headed."

"You're hungry."

"I'm OK. It was just getting up too quickly."

But Kelly knew Ella was right and that the weakness and dizziness were due to eating so little food over the last several days. He'd barely eaten since boarding the plane. He knew hunger had its own schedule, regardless of what he thought he could control. So he resolved to move and act with extra care now. Most of all, he had to do everything right to get Ella back home safely.

"I'm going to keep an eye on you," Ella said.

"Ok, I guess that's alright," Kelly said laughing as they made their way to the cabin.

The mountains were beginning to warm as the sun filtered through the thin, high clouds and reflected heat from the surface of the snow. The warmth felt good on Ella's skin and she stayed outside while Kelly went into the cabin. She knew he was gathering up the food, but she didn't want to think about that any more.

Kelly looked at his watch as he entered the cabin. It was only the second time he had done that in seven days. It was 07:45. The hours of remaining daylight were on his mind now, and they would remain so. He felt the sun's nagging urgency like the sound of breaking waves on a beach, always in the background. The ticking clock. It would frame everything he did. It didn't make him anxious but it would also not allow him to rest. The clock was a familiar companion, useful, though not always loved. He had learned to use it wisely throughout his life.

Inside the cabin, he packed all the food in the small rucksack and put both water bottles in the outside pockets. He swung the pack on his back and then walked over to the corner of the cabin and picked up the brightly colored nylon bag that held the paraglider.

He stepped outside and walked 30 feet to the center of the open area that Ella had shoveled. He dropped the bag holding the paraglider and turned toward the upper ridges of the mountains. He felt the breeze on his face. He held his arms out to his side and turned his hands out and the soft wind touched his palms.

Ella watched him. She had built a small mound of snow with the shovel and was sitting on top of it, leaning back, using it as a back rest. Her legs were outstretched and her ankles crossed. Her red jacket was wrapped tightly around her and her arms were folded across her chest. She looked at Kelly warmly, and with curiosity.

"You're up to something," she said.

"The wind is coming down the mountain but it's not that strong," Kelly said. "With any luck it will stay this way."

"I haven't really been thinking about the wind."

"There's another way for us to get out of the mountains," Kelly said. "If this glider is in good condition we can fly from here. We're high enough to make it all the way to the valley to the northwest, to the farm houses and road."

"I thought you said no more flying through the air?"

Kelly laughed. "I changed my mind."

"I do that sometimes. Do you know how this thing is supposed to work?"

"Yes, it's a tandem paraglider. There are two harnesses, once for each of us. I've done a lot of paragliding. I'm a little rusty but I know what I'm doing."

"How do you know if it's in good condition?" she asked.

"I need to inspect it. I'll check the risers and carabiners to make sure they are not badly worn, and inspect the nylon lines and the fabric for any tears or damage. We have no idea how long that thing was in that cabin but it looks well taken care of. We'll inspect the harnesses also."

Ella looked behind her to the mountain and then turned back to Kelly. "We should probably get started."

"But first, eat one of these." Kelly reached into the rucksack and handed one of the energy bars to Ella. She hesitated but then took it, removed the wrapper, and slowly took a bite. She handed the rest to Kelly.

He looked at her and shook his head.

"I'm only doing this if you are," she said.

Kelly reluctantly took the bar from her and bit a piece off. Then he handed it back to her. She ate the rest.

"How are we going to do this, to make it fly?" Ella said.

"We will need the wind to be right. It's best if it's coming up the mountains but I haven't seen it do that yet. I've been watching it. If the wind is coming down behind us, it makes it much harder. But we can still launch the paraglider if it's not too strong. We might be able to find a calm cycle. It won't be easy in the snow but we have a decent chance."

"Let's try then. I want to try," Ella said.

"If we do everything right we won't need to be as lucky."

"Are we lucky?"

"We've been lucky enough. No one can deny that."

Ella laughed. "They better not."

Kelly removed the paraglider from its bag and he and Ella each pulled one end until it was completely extended. It was shaped like the visor of a hat, slightly curved across the front and much longer than it was wide. It was more than forty feet across, with rigid plastic panels separating the open cells across the front edge where air entered when in flight, giving the wing structure. Three sets of nylon lines, one set in the back, another in the middle and one in the front, were sewn into the glider and divided at the center. They ran down each side to two central points where they ended in webbing-like loops that would be connected to the carabiner of the harnesses. Each riser had a brake, or toggle that would be used to steer simply by pulling down and slowing that side of the wing, simply by creating drag. It was the simplest form of flight.

Chapter 13

Kelly had originally intended to use the paraglider as a shelter, some protection from the wind and rain and maybe offering a little warmth, but always there was a vague notion in the back of his mind that it was also a way out of the mountains. He had flown from remote, high peaks many times before, making a fast exit from an otherwise long journey out of the mountains.

He felt good that he had carried the paraglider all the way up here. That's the best he could offer himself in terms of accolades. Their fate would rest on doing everything right and hoping for some luck. He knew that his decision—to be launching a paraglider in such a dangerous place into an unsettled sky—was filled with risk.

Still, despite understanding all this, he knew they had to try. Because the outcome was almost certain if they stayed up here. They would become too weak from hunger to survive the journey out of the mountains. And trying meant everything. Trying meant faith and courage and belief in your ability. Trying meant staying in the game.

They started together on one end of the paraglider looking for tears in the fabric and then running their fingers along the thin nylon lines to check for abrasion or cuts. Once Ella knew what to inspect, she began working her way across from the other side.

After inspecting the fabric of the wing, they checked the risers for cuts or other damage and finally the metal carabiners for corrosion and cracks. It took an hour. Kelly checked his watch. It was 0900.

"I didn't find anything. How does it look on your side?" Kelly said as he walked over to Ella's side.

"There's just one little hole, right here on the end."

Kelly reached out and held up the fabric to the sky. The hole was the diameter of a small nail and almost perfectly symmetrical.

"That's no problem. It won't affect anything. Is that all you found?

"Yes."

"Okay, that's a lot better than I thought it would be."

"It will fly?"

"With some help from us and a little luck, it'll fly like a sleigh."

Ella was feeling the effect of hunger more acutely now, but she laughed in spite of it.

"You mean like Santa's sleigh?"

"Yes. I think we'll just say it's Christmas Eve."

The two of them knelt in the snow and folded up the paraglider. They placed it back in its bag.

Then Kelly stood up and faced the high peaks again. He turned his bare palms out to the wind. He didn't feel anything on his hands but a slight breeze passed his face and the wind, as light as it was, made him anxious. It could change at any moment and become stronger. And he knew his and Ella's plan depended on timing and planning things as best they could. The light cycles of wind coming down the mountain right now weren't ideal but Kelly knew they still had a chance. If the wind became stronger, maybe five miles an hour or more, it would be impossible to launch the paraglider in the snow. They would never be able to run fast enough to create the lift that they needed.

"When can we fly?" Ella said. "We have presents to deliver."

"We're going to need a runway first."

"We'll probably need to build our own."

"It won't need to be too long, though," Kelly answered. "That's the good news. I saw a place over there." He pointed to the middle of the snowfield to the north of them. "Look, it has a gentle downhill run that drops away steeply after a hundred feet. If we pack down the snow we should be able to run fast enough to get in the air."

"What's the bad news?"

"We need to keep running until we get in the air, and before the end of the runway meets that cliff."

Ella looked at Kelly and nodded. "I'm ready to build that runway."

"We have the lucky shovels," Kelly said. He saw Ella tilt her head and give him a puzzled look.

"They just happen to be the exact thing we needed."

"Well, that's luck, giving us what we need," she said. "Thank you, luck, wherever you are."

Kelly chuckled. "I think luck is close by. Come on, let's build our runway."

They retrieved the snow shovels from the cabin and made their way to the snowfield. They stopped just uphill from a broad ramp that ran evenly downhill and then disappeared over a rise.

Kelly planted his shovel in the snow and walked downhill. He traced the outline of what would be their runway with his boots, marking the edges by dragging his feet in the snow.

Then he walked back up to where Ella was standing

"I think if we clear about a foot of the fresh snow that should be enough. Then we will need to pack down the old snow with our boots. It's long enough. We may not be off the ground until it drops away but that little dip in the slope at the end will put us in the air."

Ella turned and looked at Kelly, puzzled. He realized he was leaving something out.

"You'll be right in front of me," he said. "We have to run together at the same speed. We're hooked into the same set of attachments. Once we're in the air you'll be sitting right in front of me but a little lower. We can practice running on the launch without being attached to the paraglider."

"Okay," she answered. "I want to practice. But it's the wind, isn't it? Isn't that what we can't predict?"

"Yes. There's a chance it could switch and start coming up the mountain, in our favor—but it could keep blowing downhill and become stronger."

Kelly turned back to the mountain and felt the air with his palms and his face. The direction was the same but he felt the gusts getting stronger than before.

"The wind changes so much up here it has to be in our favor sometimes," Ella said.

Kelly paused and looked at her and then turned back to look down the mountain. Ella saw him examining the launch path. But he was thinking about what Ella had said.

Kelly continued looking down the mountain and out toward the valley. "If we're ready the moment the wind switches in our favor then everything can work," Kelly said finally.

"Then let's not worry about what the wind will do in between," Ella said.

Kelly looked at her and nodded. "That's what we'll do then," he said.

Ella had both shovels in her hands. She handed one to Kelly and they walked down the slope together to begin clearing their path.

It took them over an hour and after they'd finished that stage, the work of packing it down with their boots took almost as long.

Kelly walked back to retrieve the paraglider while Ella finished off the path. He pulled the paraglider from its bag and he and Ella stretched it out above their launch path. Then they both pulled out the two harnesses.

"Let's do a couple practice runs," Kelly said.

"How fast should we go?" Ella said.

"Medium fast for our practice runs. We won't be attached to the paraglider but we will be attached to each other so we have to run at the same speed."

"What about when we have the paraglider with us," asked Ella.

"When you start running, it's going to feel heavy, like you're pulling a plow. But it will get easier as the wing starts to come up over our heads. You just keep running as hard as you can, keep putting pressure on the harness as you gain more speed. "

Kelly showed Ella how to pull the harness over her shoulders, put her arms through the shoulder straps, and clicked the metal buckles that connected her leg loops to the harness. Then Kelly put his harness on and connected the two harnesses. He checked his watch. It was 11:00 am.

They practiced running together without being attached to the paraglider, connected to each other by nylon and metal as they worked to synchronize the pace and cadence of their stride. They stumbled in the loose snow on the first two runs, and on their third go Kelly accidentally caught Ella's right heel with his toe as they began to accelerate. They both went down in a spectacular tumble. That was their last significant mis-step. They began working it out each time. Getting better. And after several more practice runs they were moving together with little effort, like dance partners. When they finally felt like they had built the launch run sequence into their bodies' memories, and that the movements were as familiar as walking up steps, they unclipped their leg loops and took off their harnesses but left the harnesses connected. It would be more efficient to leave them connected. Kelly knew from experience that the wind sometimes gave you only a narrow window to launch a paraglider.

The two of them sat together and shared an energy bar and drank some water. And then they waited.

They both had been watching the wind. Before they started their practice runs, Kelly had cut a strip of nylon from the paragliding storage bag and tied it to the end of a wooden pole he had found at the back of the cabin. He sank the pole in the snow about ten feet below the bottom of their launch run, and a few feet off to the side. It was plainly visible from the very top of the run, where they could watch it before making the decision to sprint forward and launch. The nylon strip had immediately showed the wind. It danced with the smallest hint of a breeze. But since its erection it had been pointing downhill without fail, extending slightly sometimes, and other times standing straight out perpendicular to the pole when a stronger downslope gust caught it.

It had been natural for Kelly and Ella to look hopefully in the direction of the pole, even when they wanted to not think about it so much. But part of them believed that by looking they could will the wind to shift, if they tried hard enough. An upslope cycle that would bring them home could be borne from the grace of optimism. But after practicing their runs they knew they couldn't let themselves be held captive by that idea. The constant attention to the wind had put their nerves on edge. So now both Ella and Kelly sat above the launch run, using their harnesses as seat cushions to insulate them from the snow. The nylon strip was in their sights, but they were not fixated on it.

The practice runs had built a memory network into their muscles and nerves and established their timing, but they could not practice the speed of an actual launch run and they could not run the entire path. Their forward momentum would have been too much to slow themselves at the bottom before they reached the steep drop. For the launch that would carry them into the sky, they would have to do everything right the first time. And they would have to do it without hesitating. Completely committed. It was another reason the direction of the wind was so important. They needed things in their favor as much as possible. For that, they would have to be patient. They would have to wait.

Chapter 14

The thin nylon fabric of the paraglider stretched out behind them on the surface of the snow, rustling in the light breeze, the wing tips extending out as if it were in flight, all its colored lines running down to the paragliding harness. It was ready for flight.

It looked unremarkable lying on the snow. Its natural state was to be moving across the sky. But Ella and Kelly had not put their harnesses on yet. They could feel the prevailing wind on the bare skin on the back of their necks. It was still flowing steadily downhill. The nylon strip in front of them still held its tail straight downslope; rigid and steady rather than dancing to a varied rhythm. And it had given no indication of showing an uphill breeze. Not yet. It was 1:00.

Kelly had felt the fatigue of hunger when they were practicing their launch runs. His legs were heavy. Just walking back up to the top felt taxing on his body. But he had been keeping his focus on the present—the next few hours. As he sat in the snow, he began to consider the possibility that they would be stranded on the mountain, more than likely for an extended period, if they did not launch today. Storms were more frequent in these mountains in spring than clear skies. The break in the weather they had today was more than likely going to be gone soon. He knew that. He could see it in the wisps of thin clouds in the higher altitudes that were now appearing. Even though the present conditions held a lot of uncertainty he knew they had to take the risk. All of this was entering his mind as the hours ticked by. They needed to fly today.

Ella lifted her legs slightly while sitting on her harness and knocked her boots together several times. Then she stood up.

"My toes are getting cold, I'm just going to walk up the hill a little way, so I'm not just sitting," she called out to Kelly. Then she started climbing up the slope behind them.

She moved steadily, but not quickly, kicking deep steps in the snow.

The movement took her mind away from the waiting and the wind, and she felt the warmth generated by her body. Kelly watched her briefly and then decided to follow. They both moved slowly, bringing enough blood flow to their limbs and feet to begin to warm them.

Ella had climbed about 100 feet above the paraglider and could see the details of the lower mountain reveal themselves. The snowfields below looked bigger from here, more expansive, and extraordinarily vast. The creek that cut through them stood out as a dark blue sliver as it bent and fell with the terrain and disappeared suddenly into the forest several thousand feet below.

As she looked above to see the mountain steepen a hundred feet higher, Ella felt a strong downslope gust of wind and, though she wanted its direction to change, the sharp breeze felt good on her face. She breathed in the cold air and sank her boots deeper in the snow. Then she relaxed her legs slightly and looked downslope to see Kelly climbing in her tracks. She saw the gust of wind reach him and he stopped moving, pausing in the snow, his knees slightly bent and his body leaning into the slope. He was looking uphill now, appearing to search the mountain for something he had seen a moment before but now could not locate. Ella looked, too. Then she noticed that, in the midst of this dangerous place, something had changed. The air was completely still.

They both waited several seconds, expecting the wind to start spilling downhill again at any second. But nothing came. They looked at each other and remained silent, listening.

More seconds passed.

"The wind hasn't stopped blowing since we've been here," Ella said finally.

"Let's wait for a couple minutes."

After thirty seconds had passed, Ella put the bare palms of her hands in the air. Still not a hint of breeze. They waited another minute and then she put her palms out again.

"Do you feel anything?" she asked.

"Nothing."

Without saying anything, Ella started down the slope, moving in long, plunging strides, almost running. Kelly saw her turn and start down but he stayed put, still scanning the upper slopes, trying to detect a hint of a breeze. But nothing came. He turned to look at the streamer 100 feet below at the bottom of the launch path. It was motionless, hanging limply.

He quickly turned and began following Ella.

Kelly kept trying to catch glimpses of the streamer as he approached Ella, who was already at the paraglider. He was now almost running, or trying to run, but it was still no quicker than a fast walk in the deep snow. The streamer was now stirring again, dancing from one direction to another.

Ella was already putting on her wool beanie and red, nylon jacket. She had her harness at her feet as she unzipped its main compartment in the back and threw her water bottle inside.

Kelly quickly gathered the remaining items they had with them—including their rucksacks—and stuffed them into the cavernous compartment in the back of his harness. He zipped it closed. Ella was bringing her knees up and down quickly, marching in place to keep her muscles warm and blood flowing. She waited where the two risers lay in the snow, extended down from the paraglider lines that led up to the wing behind them. Her eyes were fixed on the streamer.

Kelly walked up the slope to the back of the paraglider and pulled the top edge of the wing backward so it formed a U shape. He then walked down each side and pulled both wing tips out to lessen the chance that one of them might get tucked under the lines when they launched. It was not a guarantee but it was one more thing they could do to put things in their favor. He then walked back to Ella and grabbed the paraglider's nylon risers.

Working each riser individually, he pulled the numerous lines apart from each other and straightened them to remove the inevitable small tangles. These could still tangle again during the launch but would likely pull free when they came under tension as Ella and Kelly pulled the wing up to begin their run. Kelly then laid the risers gently on the snow on either side of Ella and stepped behind her. He pulled his harness over his shoulders and clipped his leg loops buckles closed. Ella did the same with her harness. She ran her hands along the thick fabric of the leg loops and tugged the loops up slightly, feeling them settle against her legs. She and Kelly were now linked and for the first time flying off the mountain was no longer theoretical, but something imminent. They both felt a rush of excitement and anxiousness. Ella let her gloved hands hang on thin loops of cord sewn into the wide shoulder straps that ran over her jacket, allowing the energy in her arms and body to remain suspended, resting, but holding energy, anticipating what lay ahead.

Being buckled into their harness was a simple act of commitment. It was unquestioned that they would trust each stitch in the fabric and the engineering that went into the metal carabiners that would link them to the paraglider. Their trust in the paraglider itself was more instinctive; they had already seen how it rested on the ground and lifted itself in a gentle breeze, and they knew that it only needed enough speed to get it off the ground and it would fly. They could visualize that as they looked down their launch ramp toward the expanse of valleys below. This was their way out of the mountains.

"Check all your buckles once more and make sure they're all locked, and leg loops tight," Kelly said.

After a few seconds, Ella responded, "Yes, I'm all set."

Kelly clipped their harnesses into the paraglider risers and shut the carabiner gates. Ella heard the metallic click of the carabiner gates and took a breath. Her eyes were fixed on the streamer. She settled into the center of her body and shifted her feet slightly, rotating them in the snow and adjusting her footing. Her mind and body were synched. She was ready.

But there was still the wind, the only aspect they could not control. And it was indifferent to every step in their preparation and any effort they would make for their own survival. It was now gusting downslope in sporadic bursts of about ten miles an hour.

Both Kelly and Ella felt it on the back of their necks and they heard the top of the wing ruffle and saw it get pushed back on itself. One of them would have to unclip from the paraglider and pull the wing back and lay it out flat again.

It was 3 p.m. and they both could sense the sky was changing. It was losing its clarity and turning opaque at the higher altitudes.

Another gust of wind came from behind and the nylon fabric rustled loudly. Kelly felt his body tense.

He unclipped from Ella and the paraglider but kept his harness on and walked back up to the top of the paraglider. He pulled the fabric back and extended the two wingtips, clearing the lines that had become tangled.

Then he saw Ella looking up at him. "We still have a chance," he said.

"I know."

"I'm going to wait up here for a minute. I want these downhill cycles of wind to stop."

Ella settled into her boots and shook her shoulders and arms to keep blood flowing in her body. She and Kelly both felt the air getting cooler.

She looked downslope and saw the streamer was barely moving. But Kelly didn't trust it and he remained behind the glider. Ella glanced up at him and her eyes quickly caught the white, dust-like cloud on the high face of the mountains behind him. It was at least a thousand feet above them and was flowing down like a curtain over the rock face, obscuring parts of it at first but expanding, making the broad face below it disappear. It almost looked harmless, just a line of white powdery snowy pillows.

Chapter 15

Before she could shout a warning to Kelly, the sound reached them. It was a building thunder, a massive wave crashing on a distant beach. But the avalanche was moving closer and getting louder all the time.

"Run to your right, Ella!" Kelly yelled. "I'll pick up the wing."

She didn't wait. She ran diagonally downhill into soft snow and sunk to her knees, but she drew on all the strength she had and it was enough to push herself through it, bracing herself with her arms and swinging them forward, driving and balancing her body. She was running from the avalanche knowing only that it was somewhere behind them.

Kelly bunched up the paraglider and began running too, dragging it across the surface of the snow, keeping it off the ground as much as possible, just enough to not pull on Ella.

They made it about 100 feet before the blast of air hit them and sent them off their feet into a cloudy world that had no references, other than the visceral pull of gravity. Kelly saw the far ridgeline disappear as the air threw him forward and he felt the terrifying freedom of release from gravity. As his body flew, he waited for what would happen next.

They tumbled through the snow, feeling every fraction of every second. All they could see was white. There was no sky or ridges, not even the white snowfield below them. They heard only the consuming roar of the avalanche until their bodies finally came to rest, buried partially in the snow. And suddenly it was quiet.

Ella heard her own rapid breaths, and Kelly's gasps and coughs. She felt the cold press of snow on her face and realized she was pointed downhill. Her harness had ridden up her back and she felt its strain in her leg loops. She shifted her hips and tried rolling downhill onto her back but felt something pulling on her left leg. She pulled her leg up toward her chest and looked down to see several of the paraglider lines wrapped around her lower leg. She pulled up again, this time harder, and felt some of the lines release. She slid her legs downhill and sat up awkwardly and braced herself against the slope with both arms, the harness now offering some support. She believed she was OK, but wondered if it was true. Then Kelly appeared above her, his long brown hair and eyebrows matted with snow.

"I like your hair," Ella said.

"Is it still there?"

"Yes, only it's white now, and a little messy."

"Don't move yet. Does anything hurt?"

"No. I think I'm OK."

Kelly stepped down to Ella's feet and unwrapped the remaining paraglider lines from her leg. He unclipped her from the paraglider and helped her sit up with her back against the slope of the hill.

It took them a good thirty minutes to untangle the paraglider's lines and reorganize their equipment, which included finding their hats, sunglasses and gloves. The wind streamer and its pole had been in the main path of the avalanche and Kelly guessed they now lay over a thousand feet below them, buried under about twenty feet of snow. The 100 feet that he and Ella had run before the avalanche hit them had put them on the periphery of its course. They had experienced mostly the blast of air.

The landscape had been drastically changed by the avalanche. Several feet of snow had been scoured from the slope, to within a few inches of the ground's rocky surface. The snow had been so cleanly and uniformly removed that it looked as though a giant broom had swept it down the mountain.

As Kelly and Ella walked back up to the top of their launch path, they saw the snow underneath their boots was now hard and stable, making walking easy. The area around them had the eerie feel of a clean ice rink, but with hidden dangers. About 100 feet below them, a truck-sized rock outcrop had appeared.

As they traversed the slope, their boots crunched in the thin snow and the wind blew directly in their faces, sweeping across the slope now rather than coming downhill. And it was blowing steadily, at about ten miles an hour. Kelly's throat tightened and he felt the familiar hollowness in the pit of his stomach. A wind that strong and steady indicated more stormy weather. And the day was getting late. If this wind was coming uphill, it would at least give them a chance. But it was even stronger than before and still in the wrong direction.

Kelly dropped the paraglider in the snow and removed his harness. The wind caught the edges of the paraglider and the fabric snapped and ruffled with each gust. The sky continued to darken.

Neither of them spoke for several minutes. Ella gazed down the slope towards the valley, the long, clean snowfield—vacant and endless—now a reminder of their situation. A series of events had taken place that were beyond their control. The mountains were ambivalent to their situation and both of them knew that, but it didn't feel that way.

Ella glanced over at Kelly. He met her eyes and then turned and began walking to the far end of the avalanche path. He seemed to walk with no apparent purpose, Ella thought. He was just walking so he could free his mind of something. She sat on her harness and watched him walking up the slope and then down a little way, and then back up. Finally, she stood and began making short sprints down the hill, as though she was practicing the launch they would do with the paraglider, the one that would take them safely home, to rest and food. Practicing just to practice. She couldn't think of anything else to do and in a way it maintained her belief that they would fly off the mountain.

Kelly saw her and knew the chances of getting her out of these mountains was now painfully small. He felt panic rise from his chest and it embarrassed him and he forced it away. But his legs suddenly felt heavy, his body responding to their reality. Then he said it aloud to himself, quietly, to make it real. "We will find a way out."

Yet he knew he and Ella were too weak to walk down through the deep snow. They would have to stay a little longer. They would need to hold on. Maybe there would be a short window, a break in the weather over the next two days. It was possible, though he knew storms like this don't just come and go in one day. He and Ella would be another day weaker tomorrow. Would they die here? The question intruded into his thoughts for just a second or two before he pushed it away. He knew it was possible; that they could remain trapped up here and become too weak to walk out. But it was not inevitable. And he believed dying up here was more likely the moment they stopped believing they would escape the mountains.

Neither of them wanted to keep waiting – waiting for some luck, waiting for the wind to change, waiting to see what the mountains would eventually do with them. At least the moving, the walking and running, helped keep their minds free, if only a little.

Kelly turned and had begun walking back to Ella when a gust of wind caught the flap of his jacket and its metal zipper smacked him sharply across the mouth. Usually he would have cursed, but now he was only curious to know how such a small zipper could hurt that much.

Ella had finished another short sprint down the hill and was walking back up the slope when she saw Kelly making his way to the top of the launch path.

"It's easier running now with the soft snow gone," she called.

Kelly nodded and smiled. "Just don't wear yourself out."

"It's like track practice at school," she said.

It did look like a running track, Kelly thought. And he kicked the toes of his boots into the snow and felt the firm surface under his feet. The dry crystals that had been buried deep all winter, scattered off the surface, cold and light, carried through the air by the wind. Kelly paused and looked at the slope below. Then he turned and looked behind him while slowly walking backwards, still gauging the angle of the slope, the wind strong in his face.

Fragments of an idea were shifting in his mind as he considered a new possibility.

And then the parts assembled themselves, each connecting to and depending on the other, to build an image in his mind as real as the snow that Kelly was standing on.

He knelt down on one knee and looked more closely at the slope, as though sighting along the gunwales of a ship, assessing its seaworthiness. First the angle of the slope in front of him and then turning to look at the angle below.

Ella had stopped running and was watching him.

"Let's bring the glider over to this side of the path and lay it out parallel to the slope," he said finally.

"You're thinking of something."

"We're going to launch sideways, into the wind."

Ella looked at Kelly, wondering if she had heard him correctly. She remained there, head slightly cocked, waiting for him to repeat what he had just said. But she only saw him pause briefly to look again at the slope below them. Then he began walking quickly to the top of the launch path. Ella followed him.

They picked up the paraglider and carried it to the near side of the path, and set it down. The wind whipped the fabric into the air but Ella helped Kelly control it by tucking it under in places and untangling the lines. She then grabbed the harnesses and placed them on top of the glider to keep it from being lifted by the gusts. Most of their gear was already packed away in the harnesses.

The paraglider was roughly pointed into the wind but not toward the reassuring open space above the downhill slope. It was contrary to everything that Kelly had taught Ella about launching a paraglider. But whatever questions Ella had about this plan, she quickly dismissed. She sensed in Kelly's urgency the promise of something that could have them flying.

There was renewed commitment between them now, even though they had not discussed his idea. Ella trusted him and she knew they had to move quickly. She glanced upward and could see the sky continuing to change. They could both feel the palpable danger the building darkness held. Ella felt thirst rising in her throat but she wasn't concerned about that right now.

The wind had lessened to about five miles an hour but they both knew it was a brief lull. It would likely increase again soon, and continue to increase.

"Zip your jacket all the way up and put your hat and gloves on," Kelly said.

Ella retrieved her hat and gloves from her jacket pockets and zipped its front. Kelly already had his harness in his hands and quickly swung the straps over his shoulders. He reached down and clipped his two leg loops closed.

Ella backed up to him, pulled her harness on and reached down and grabbed her leg straps. She swung them up and around her thighs and closed the buckles. She and Kelly connected the harnesses to each other.

Then Kelly turned to face the paraglider. He reached down and picked up the two risers that anchored all of the paraglider's lines.

Holding the risers to his front, he reversed them by flipping the one in his right hand above the one in his left hand, and brought the left one under and to the right.

Ella continued facing the wind with her back to Kelly. The lull had allowed the fabric of the paraglider to remain quiet, but new gusts were sweeping over them and the fabric was now coming alive again.

"The wind is picking up," said Ella.

"We're almost there."

"What should I do when you lift the wing up? We can't run down the path in this wind."

But Kelly didn't respond. He carefully completed connecting himself and Ella to the paraglider. Then he closed and locked the metal carabiner gates. And then checked them again.

Ella took a deep breath and exhaled. She shuffled her boots to feel the solid snow underneath her and looked up at the changing sky. It was now dark blue, steel-like, behind the clouds to the west. She felt the dryness rise in her throat but she still turned her head and spat. She was ready.

Kelly pulled the upper set of lines on each riser and the fabric opened to the wind. It snapped like a rifle shot. The paraglider sprang to life, its chambers instantly filling with air and shooting both wing tips to the sides. He kept the paraglider on the ground by pulling on the lower set of lines. It was no longer just fabric and lines; it was a wing and it wanted to be above the ground and it fought Kelly to be there—to lift and to meet the wind. It took all of Kelly's skill and strength to keep it down.

"When I pull it up it's going to pull me forward about ten feet. Really fast," he told Ella.

"I'll run backwards with you."

"Just like we talked about but couldn't practice."

"I'm attached to you," she reminded him. "I'll go as fast as you do."

"Match my speed."

"Yes."

"Once we have the wing overhead and it's stable, I'll tell you what to do. We're going to run straight into the wind for about twenty feet and then slowly start to shuffle sideways and then turn and sprint downhill. I'll tell you when."

"We're going to run sideways?"

"Shuffle sideways. Like a crab. The wind will keep the wing in the air so we don't need to run fast until we turn downhill—and then we'll lose the wind."

"OK. I'll shuffle like a crab."

"Yes, good. Just remember you're in front so I am following you. The transitions need to be gradual."

"I got it."

"How do you feel?"

She smiled. "I feel like a strong crab in the sand."

"Perfect."

A gust of wind rolled unseen off the far ridgeline, following the smooth contours of the slope, the cold air heavy and descending unhindered. There was not a single tree to disrupt it or give notice of its arrival. It quickly swept across the broad snowfield and then over Ella and Kelly and into the fabric of the wing. It caught enough of the wing to jerk both of them sharply back about ten feet. Kelly kept the wing on the ground by pulling and holding the lower set of lines.

"That was strong," Ella said.

"We could get something stronger."

"I hope not."

Ella tilted her head back and looked at the sky. She inhaled deeply through her nose and then slowly exhaled as she brought her head down, pushing the air out of her lungs and letting her arms hang by her side. She inhaled again, watching the far ridgeline. Then she clenched her fists and shook her hands loose, exhaling deeply.

Kelly was watching the fabric in front of him. His vision and hearing intently focused on the wind.

A series of weaker gusts swept over them. Between the gusts, Ella pumped her legs, bringing her knees quickly to her chest to stay warm. They could only wait, poised and anxious, for a smooth cycle of wind.

Chapter 16

Finally, it came.

Ella felt it first, an even flow meeting her face. It was smooth like the flow of water coming over the lip of a dam. It was predictable. And that's exactly what Kelly was waiting for.

The wing came up sharply with Kelly's quick snap up of the leading-edge lines and it pulled them both forward with tremendous force, almost faster than Kelly could react to. But it stopped just as quickly as he pulled the rear lines and checked its surge. The wing quickly found its balance with the wind. It was now in the air. Kelly controlled its surging and shifting by alternately pulling and releasing the sets of rear and upper lines. Ella moved with him as he adjusted his position, matching the wing's movement. Kelly sensed the wind through the paraglider, and after he had kept it stationary for several seconds he spun 180 degrees to his left and with that turn the risers straightened. He was now looking directly at Ella and the narrow width of the launch path in front of them. He glanced above him and saw the wing fully inflated and the lines free of any tangles.

He peered over the top of Ella's head to the far ridgeline. There he saw the wind kick off a curtain of snow from its lip. It sped toward him and Ella in narrow, silvery wisps.

"Let's move forward a couple steps," Kelly said. "There's going to be a lot of resistance but just keep pushing."

"Okay."

"I think things are on our side."

Ella glanced at her hair whipping in the wind off her right shoulder. "Yes, I think so, too," she said.

Then she stepped forward and immediately felt the energy of the wind against her. She instinctively lowered her shoulders and dug the toes of her boots into the snow, driving her legs against the wind. Kelly did the same and together they began moving, inching forward only as the pulse and ebb of the wind allowed. As they moved, they balanced themselves on the slope against the shifting paraglider above them, which was alternately pulling sideways and pushing backwards.

Within a few steps, they had gained momentum and the resistance against the wind decreased. The steps came faster and their progress was now undeniable.

"Two more steps and we're running downhill," shouted Kelly.

"I'm ready!"

They were both bent into the wind, their upper bodies leaning forward as one. Their feet kicked into the snow, sending fragments flying in their wake. Some larger pieces landed on the slope and rolled rapidly downhill on the hard snowpack. The wing overhead surged and fell back as the wind gusted more strongly.

"Turn right!"

"Yes!"

Ella turned and accelerated downhill. With no resistance from the wind, she gained speed and momentum. Kelly stayed with her stride for stride and cast his eyes upward to see how the wing was responding. He felt it before he saw it—the loss of energy in the wing as the airflow left it. He saw the middle of the wing sag.

"Faster, Ella!"

Ella felt her shoulder straps go slack, almost weightless, as if the paraglider above them was suddenly gone. She thought maybe it had somehow become unattached. But Kelly's voice behind her and the sudden freedom from resistance was all she needed. She was now sprinting, trusting that whatever was happening with the wing would be fixed if she did just one thing—run as fast as she could. So that's what she did.

The wing sagged more, but then billowed again, suspended between flight and collapse. Kelly saw it for a fraction of a second but he knew he didn't need to see it—he could feel it. And in the pit of his stomach, a deep echo sent the bleak message to his conscious brain: it would be the end If they failed here. Their momentum would send them over the 50-foot rock bench that was now just a short distance in front of them.

The sudden jerk at the front of the harness told Kelly that he was quickly being pulled downslope. It added one more piece to the shifting events that he was a part of but unable to completely control. Only his instincts would make a difference now, but they had to be right, and they had to respond without hesitation. Ella was accelerating and Kelly stumbled trying to match her sudden speed. His chest and head flew forward and his right knee dropped into the snow. He knew he was falling. Ella felt it too, and it pulled her back. She pushed harder into the harness, the nylon straps biting into her shoulders. But Kelly continued down, out of balance, his face close to the snow, and with his next stride he saw the heel of Ella's left boot inches from his jaw. Her boot kicked up snow and he inhaled it, the icy cold staggering his breath. Bent over, and with only the steep slope keeping him upright, he used all the strength he had in his left leg to counter the force of gravity that was trying to kill him. Because he knew it would kill Ella, too.

But it didn't feel possible to stay upright. The propulsion toward the ground was so great. He felt his left leg buckle, but it held instead, and then he managed a slight push up. It was enough! He stumbled forward and his right leg lurched forward. He planted it firmly in the snow and pushed hard.

All their energy was now descending into the steepest part of the launch, their weight and momentum bent into the harness, carrying them past the point where they could stop. Rushing downhill, they were completely committed.

The sudden speed brought the wing back to life and it snapped loudly as it regained its shape, the wind rushing in from the front and lifting the leading edge. They were outrunning the wind. The slight lift through the harness that neither of them immediately understood, but sensed in the lightness of their feet. The heavy pull of the wing was now lifting them and they felt their feet reaching for the ground, but mostly finding air. Then the ground dropped away and the rocks of the cliff that had menaced them were below, shrinking, and harmless.

The sudden rush of wind met their skin and its sound swept over them and became the voice of their departure. It was as wild and loud as the roar of the creek below them crashing onto boulders on its way down the mountain. With her hands reaching toward the sky, Ella sent a wild yell across the basin below. It reached the rocks of the upper ridges and then echoed and came back down the mountain, settling softly in the air a few hundred feet above the snow.

Grey and black pillows of moisture were building in the sky in front of them and Ella and Kelly felt the turbulence as it jerked them up occasionally or pulled them sideways. A slight updraft boosted them skyward and Kelly steered the glider toward the broad, open valley to the northwest. In the distance, thousands of feet below, a farmhouse and a long, straight country road were visible in the valley, the gateway to civilization. He could see the green fields of early spring grass.

Above her, Ella saw a long, flickering shape against the grey sky. Kelly hadn't noticed it. She pointed at it with her fingers spread wide, her palm extended broadly. Kelly knew the gesture was not a casual observation. It was an instruction. There was something up there in the sky with them, on the journey with them, and Ella wanted to meet it.

Now he saw the shape against the building clouds and steered the glider to the right, angling in the flowing air in a direction that might bring them closer. But it would be by chance that their paths would cross as they were both moving with the air currents, shifting left and right, sometimes rising skyward in columns of light air and sometimes sinking in pockets of heavier air.

But Ella maintained a fix on the shape, her hand periodically pointing and waving to make sure Kelly had not lost sight of it. He thought there was a chance they would reach it. He saw Ella look up, turn to look at Kelly and nod her head. She was sure they would.

But then the glider dropped quickly in a column of sinking air and the shape moved higher and drifted quickly to the right, like driftwood rising and sinking in an ocean current. Kelly lost sight of it. They were on different trajectories now, with too much space and distance and too much chance working against them. They and the shape were moving in a three-dimensional world, and to Kelly it seemed ever out of reach. He steered the glider back to a more direct path down to the broad valley below.

It would have been impossible for Kelly to miss what Ella did next. With her arms reaching in front of her she began sweeping them out to the side and then back, fingers and palms outstretched, as though she was swimming. Kelly looked out toward the valley, unsure for the first time since they left the ground if he was doing everything right.

Then Ella pointed directly overhead and shouted.

"Up there!"

The long red ribbon was about 100 feet above them and a little to their right. When Kelly saw it he thought it looked suspended in the turbulent air by an invisible thread, anchored in the sky. But he could feel the violent movement of the air and knew both the ribbon and the glider were rising and shifting rapidly. Still, the ribbon hung there before them.

Ella was pointing and yelling. Kelly pulled both brake toggles down sharply, not far enough to slow the glider very much, but enough to create immediate lift.

Ella felt the heaviness of gravity pull on her body as the glider shot up. The air was becoming more turbulent and it rushed past her skin, but it wasn't cold like she expected. Then the ribbon appeared directly in front of her and she reached out. Just then it swept past her to the right, but her hand was already there and her fingers closed gently around it. She let out a loud whoop of excitement, held the ribbon above her head and then turned to look at Kelly. He smiled broadly, even as he worked both brake toggles, pulling and releasing, managing the wing and its constant movement in the violent air.

Ella turned and lifted herself slightly in the harness to face Kelly. With both hands, she gently threaded the ribbon through one of the metal carabiners above their heads, and tied it there. The ribbon danced in the wind and caught the sun's light, reflecting and spinning. Ella turned back to the front, lifted both arms toward the valley and kicked her legs in a rhythm that seemed to keep time with the rising and sinking air.

Searching for a landmark in the valley below, Kelly saw the roof of a large building miles in the distance, probably a barn, he thought. He aimed the glider towards it.

The snowfield below passed quickly as the terrain became steeper, dropping away in bounds. Kelly heard the crashing stream as it fell onto boulders. The world below was mesmerizing. Then his eyes caught a narrow place in the stream that somehow seemed familiar. The wind, rushing past his face, went silent, and he could only hear the sounds of the water. He looked back to the valley, found the roof of the barn and in the corner of his eye, saw the ribbon dancing in the light. A memory of climbing among the rocks and snowfields in early winter played in his consciousness, the vibrant images scrolling through his memory – the horizon of wild and remote summits and narrow ridges reaching to the sky, the blaze of a Fireweed blossom alive in the cold, high peaks, thriving by virtue of its own insistence to be there. He grasped both brake toggles with his right hand and steered the glider just with that hand, dropping his left hand to his thigh and letting it rest there. His palm facing out across his thigh, all the tendons and muscles and joints of his hand relaxed with the rhythm of his breathing. He looked down at his hand unconsciously and felt it resting, in sync with his breathing, no longer tense. The sensation of his breathing and vision and his resting hand in harmony, felt familiar to Kelly, something found that had been lost, and his mind let them exist as they were, unbound, for the first time in ten years. He looked out to the valley and saw Ella's left arm raised diagonally to the sky, her palm facing up and fingers spread, the sun reflecting off her jacket in gentle waves of red as the sound of the thundering creek below rose and fell with the pitching terrain.

"Hello there creek! "Ella yelled out as the paraglider rose slightly and then settled into a gentle glide toward the valley.

※ ※ ※

Chapter 17

The old pickup truck, its blue and green paint faded and pale from decades in the sun at this high elevation, could be seen a half mile away, speeding down the long, straight dirt road. It was raising small clouds of fine dust that rose quickly before being carried in the breeze to a large field to the truck's right. The field was vibrant green with a layer of short, thick grass. Water was rushing in a narrow irrigation ditch that separated the road and the field; the water pushing over the young grass growing close to the bank of the ditch.

The truck began to slow. And then came to a stop in the middle of the empty road. For several miles on both sides of the road only fence-lined fields and a few scattered farmhouses and barns could be seen. In some of the fields cattle were grazing. No other vehicle could be seen on the road.

The old man behind the wheel of the truck was wearing scuffed leather boots and a brown cowboy hat, its brim dark and sweat-stained. His weathered, tan face held several deep creases. He turned the truck's ignition off and sat still for half a minute, looking intently through the truck's windshield, directly ahead and up toward the sky. Then he got out of the truck and walked to its front, leaving the door open.

He stood in the middle of the road, looking up to the sky, unconcerned that anyone else might be travelling on the road. He watched a dark object in the sky gradually get larger, sometimes moving lower. Sometimes it appeared to enter the clouds near the mountains behind it, which were still dark and grey from the storm that had swept over them the last two days. Above the valley the sky was more broken, with patches of light, and in some places blue sky appeared. The old man thought the object might be a very large eagle, mostly because nothing else made sense to him. But it was too far away to tell for sure. He knew it was too small to be an aircraft. His instincts told him it was something that he should take notice of. He watched it move across the sky to his right and gradually he lost sight of it as it grew smaller and seemed to disappear in the clouds. He returned to his truck, started the engine, and continued down the road.

The truck moved across the broad valley for the better part of the afternoon on a series of long, straight roads, edging its way closer to the mountains to the southwest. The old man stopped periodically to examine the flow of water in the irrigation ditches and the gates that the water ran through. Occasionally he removed debris from the ditch. Late in the afternoon the truck finally came to the only road that ran directly toward the base of the high peaks where a sprawling farmhouse sat at the road's end. The truck turned onto the road, a cloud of dust still trailing it. From a distance it was evident the farmhouse had been built at the top of a gradual rise where the valley began to meet the base of the mountains. The farmhouse commanded a view of the valley in front of it and the high peaks behind it

It was two stories, with a gabled roof that ran down from its peak to a covered front porch that extended across the entire front of the house. Three dormers jutted out from the roof on the second floor. The porch itself was flush with the surrounding grounds and large wooden beams ran from the front of the porch to its roof. A bicycle and several long, wooden planter boxes with red and white flowers sat under the porch roof. Several pairs of work boots and tennis shoes sat on the flat stone of the porch.

A two-story barn with large sliding doors facing the road stood off the right of the farmhouse. A circular dirt driveway ran in front of the barn and then to the farmhouse.

The pickup truck slowed as it came up the driveway and parked in front of the barn. The old man stepped out of the truck and walked toward the front of the farmhouse. He stopped once and gazed toward the high peaks for several seconds before continuing.

As he reached the porch, he heard the faint sound of hooves striking the ground. It was the sound of more than one horse, he knew. He turned and looked toward the valley.

He saw two riders on horseback in the distant field, moving alongside each other, then one falling in behind the other as the horses dropped into a dry creek bed, kicking up dust as they slowed at the berm above the creek bed. He recognized the light brown coats and dark manes of the two horses even from a football field away.

The riders fell below the berm and then reappeared quickly as the horses climbed the near side of the creek bed. Both horses quickened their pace as they reached level ground, their broad shoulders and powerful legs easily finding a rhythmic gallop.

The lead rider wore a red and black flannel shirt and faded jeans. She was about forty years old and her long blond hair was tied in a ponytail that rose and fell off her right shoulder as the horses continued across the field toward the farmhouse. A young girl, 15-years old, rode behind the first horse. Her long, light brown hair draped down her cheeks and fell onto her elbows, which were cocked at her side, holding the reins of her horse. She wore scuffed cowboy boots and a burnt orange baseball cap, its visor faded with dust and sweat stained.

The old man smiled and began walking to a hitching rail that was set in the rough, short-cropped grass at the edge of the farmhouse grounds.

The two riders reined their horses to a sudden stop in front of the rail.

"Hi dad!" the woman yelled as she swung off her horse and led it to the rail.

"You two can ride with the best of them," the old man said.

"We had a good teacher," the woman said, smiling. "He was kind of stubborn but he knew what he was doing." The old man laughed as he took the reins of the young girl's horse.

"Grandpa, do you remember when I was five years old?" the girl said as she swung off the horse.

"That was when you got fast, I could no longer keep up with you," he said.

"You remember that year?" the girl asked.

"I sure do."

The old man wrapped the reins of the horse twice around the hitching rail.

"Then you remember Ella," the girl said, smiling.

The old man paused. "Ella?" he said softly. He cocked his head and looked at the girl.

"You remember her, grandpa?"

The old man nodded to the girl and looked toward the mountains behind the farmhouse.

"The little girl who lost her parents in the mountains," he said. "I remember that day like yesterday. The hikers who found her brought her out on that trail right up there," he said, pointing to a gradual ridgeline that led into the mountains. "She spent the night right in this house. Doctor Ramsey came over and checked on her and said she was dehydrated and cold but he said it was fine for her to stay here, if that's what she wanted to do. She slept in your bedroom with you. We checked on her throughout the night."

"Where do you think Ella is now?" the girl asked.

"I don't know sweetheart. I don't know where she is now. But I hope she is having a good life."

"Dad, you don't need to worry about Ella," the woman said. "She is doing just fine. You will see for yourself tonight at dinner."

The old man turned to his daughter, his weathered face registered his surprise, almost disbelief. She walked up to him and put her hand on his shoulder.

"Dad, Ella flew out of the mountains today in a paraglider with that Army Captain who was missing in the plane crash. They landed at Linnie Jones' place."

The old man took off his hat. "That can't be...with that storm we had," he said, looking to the mountains. "How did they make it?"

"The found a cabin very high in the mountains and stayed there. But they had very little food."

"We need to go get them," the old man said, turning toward the truck. "It was them that I saw earlier today."

"It's okay, grandpa," the girl said. "The search and rescue people came over to Linnie's and the Army Captain showed them on the map where the plane crash was. The Army flew up there with a helicopter and found it."

"Linnie is going to bring them both over here in about an hour," the woman said, smiling. "Ella remembers you. We told her she could stay here as long as she liked."

"Well, I just can't believe it," the old man said.

"Let's make a big dinner, grandpa," the girl said, smiling.

"We have enough time to run into town," the old man said.

"We'll come with you dad," the woman said.

The girl untied the reins of the two horses and began leading them quickly to the barn.

"I wrote down all the kinds of food they like," the girl said. "I'll meet you at the truck!"

"We'll get everything," the old man said.

"It's going to be one fine dinner, grandpa!" the girl yelled out.

The small patches of blue sky were opening more broadly now as the old man and his daughter walked quickly to the truck. A bright shaft of sunlight fell onto the barn doors as the girl approached them and she felt a radiant warmth meet her hands as she pushed them open and led the horses inside.

About the author

The author writes from his home in the Pacific Northwest, where he hikes, runs, and climbs in the mountains he first explored as a teenager.